SUMMER TIDE

PART ONE

THE KOTTOW TREE

CHAPTER ONE

It began with a rustling in the leaves, as of a brisk wind passing through. Were this *shivering* and *susurrating* a product of the wind, though, one might imagine it would start near the top of the Tree — up where the winds flew fierce and unimpeded.

But it began near the bottom. Rarely was *this* part of the Tree disturbed, for the great, gnarled trunk was so broad, it would take you a few minutes to walk all the way around it, even at a smart pace; and the boughs hung thick and heavy, like ranks of soldiers formed up against the wind, the rain, and every other disturbance the varied seasons might bring.

Mother Gantry noticed it first. Having no head for heights (she said), she had chosen an abode only some few feet off the ground; and unlike some of her more daring neighbours, her dwelling was neatly enclosed, all the way inside the trunk. Her door, tightly woven from fallen twigs and painted a sprightly red, caught the eye of every passer-by, naturally making Mother Gantry the first to espy —

and greet — all visitors to the Tree. She saw herself as something of a Headwoman to the folk who dwelt there.

The door in question, having remained firmly shut against the chill of an early spring morning, flew suddenly open with a *boot*, and bounced against the trunk.

Mother Gantry appeared, hands on her ample hips. 'What's afoot?' she called.

A face appeared among the branches above. 'Nowt, Mother Gantry.' It was Diggory Stokey, one of the folk who took up a more perilous situation (some might say) out upon the boughs. 'Don't worrit yerself.'

'I felt something,' she insisted, glaring up at his apple-round face and its cheery mop of fair hair. 'Something went all a-shake.'

Diggory shook his head. 'Just a puff of wind, Mother. Why, 'tis lucky you live so far down. What would you be like, farther up?' A rustle of leaves came — oak, near the bottom, for the most part — and Diggory's face withdrew.

Disgruntled, Mother Gantry began to shut her door — bidding fair to slam it soundly, misliking the carpenter's dismissive tone — but then it came again: a great, rustling wave among the leaves, and a profound *shiver* in the living wood of the floor. She felt it through her toes, and halfway up her legs.

The floor heaved, once.

'Oh, my,' puffed Mother Gantry, and shot out a hand, to steady herself against the knotted whorl of the doorframe.

Diggory Stokey's face reappeared. 'Come to think of it, that was a bit of a shake.'

'As I *told* thee!'

The rustling intensified, and Mother Gantry braced herself; but it was only Diggory Stokey, manoeuvring his stoutish frame, and all his carpenter's muscles, down from the boughs above. He came down the stairway — no real steps in truth, but a sequence of knots and other protrusions that spiralled around the trunk, by way of which a sure-footed soul might venture up and down. Taking up a stance upon one of the mighty lower boughs (thicker around than he was himself) that framed Mother Gantry's doorway, he cast his eyes out over the town, just as she had.

And just as she had, he saw nothing untoward. The Tree grew on the outer edge of a town called Kottow, a prosperous enough place, with its wool-merchants and its markets and whatnot. In finer weather, the *clip-clop* of horses' hooves could be heard all day long, down near the bottom of the Tree, and occasionally, a raucous shout or a smatter of laughter from those who streamed in and out of the gates.

Gawkers were commonplace, though not among the residents of Kottow. For them, the Tree's presence was as unremarkable as that of St. Mary's church — even if the Tree did rather dwarf that holy establishment, spire and all. But those who came for the markets, to trade or to buy, often veered away from the gates, and came riding or trudging up to take a gander.

Mother Gantry was a dab hand with a broom, when it came to that; some folk had no manners about them, and would poke their faces into a good woman's kitchen without so much as a by-your-leave. But if she or Diggory imagined that some hoard of curious onlookers might be the cause of the disturbance, they were proven mistaken: Kottow dozed, tranquil and at peace, a thin mist curling silently about its thatched roof-tops. Not *there* could the cause be found.

'Odd,' pronounced Diggory, and sat down upon the bough.

Just in time, for the shaking came again, and this third time was worse than the rest. If the floor of Mother Gantry's kitchen had heaved before, now it *bucked*, and rolled like a ship at sea. A rain of leaves came wafting down — oak and chestnut and elm, and even some of the birch-leaves from higher up.

A few acorns and chestnuts, left over from the autumn, fell with a sharp *crack*; and to Mother Gantry's amazed eyes, they were followed by a clutter of berries, rowan or blackthorn; wild apples, the meagre, sour kind; golden-pink medlar fruit; plums; apple-blossom; cherries and cherry-flowers, all mixed up together; and so on. It was as though the Tree were whisking through all its Seasons at once, or perhaps shedding itself of the vestiges of many Seasons past.

Diggory Stokey, having saved himself from a fall by a timely clutching at the trunk, met Mother Gantry's gaze with wide eyes. 'I could swear I saw a root come up, jus' then.'

'A root?' The word emerged sharply, like a whiplash, for Mother Gantry felt something profound and irreversible on the approach; something she did *not* like, for it meant Change, and hers was a heart that far preferred a comfortable stability. 'Roots do not come *up*, Diggory Stokey. Roots go *down*. That's their nature. What would a Tree-root want with fresh air, I ask thee?'

'I don't know,' said Diggory, ashen-faced. 'But there it goes again.'

Mother Gantry turned her head, and got an eye-full of a fine sight. Diggory was right. Up came a great, winding, gnarly Tree-root, shedding damp earth every which way, and filling the air with the scent of a freshly-dug garden. Long and wizened and stout around, this root; as it would have to be, to hold steady, with its brethren, a Tree the size of a small village.

Down it went again, into the earth, where it belonged — but not quite in the same place as it had come up.

There were more. Several went sky-high at once, thrashed about in the air, and plunged down again — and there came the heaving of the floor, a *rolling* movement, and the shaking and shuddering of the leaves.

A medlar fell past Mother Gantry's nose.

By this time, of course, the fact that something untoward was afoot had reached the attention of those farther up the tree. Mother Gantry heard the clamour of raised voices, even some shouting. Somebody's boot sailed down, and bounced.

'Quiet, the lot of ye!' Mother Gantry called. 'I cannot think with such noise!'

'T'ain't much use to go thinking,' Diggory Stokey said. 'There's only one thing this can be.'

'You keep your lips *closed*, Diggory Stokey,' Mother Gantry said. 'It's of no use looking for trouble, neither.'

'The Tree's on the move,' said Diggory stubbornly.

'No,' said Mother Gantry, and if ever catastrophe could be warded off by mere stoutness of heart it would be now, with that one, firm syllable.

'And it's about time,' he added, regaining his seat upon the bough, but with his broad back braced against the trunk. 'Folk hereabouts've been calling it the Kottow Tree, and you *know* that ain't right.'

The Tree, in fact, had been stationary a long while; perhaps since Mother Gantry was a girl, though nobody could get a straight answer out of her on *that* subject. 'The Tree likes Kottow,' she said, disappearing back into her kitchen. 'And so do I.'

The red door slammed; Mother Gantry took refuge somewhere within.

Diggory Stokey stayed out upon the bough, watching as Kottow, slowly, but with gaining speed, passed by upon the left. He liked Kottow, too, and the town liked him; he had a thriving carpentry-business, what with the residents of the Tree and those of the town, and his heart sank at the prospect of leaving it all behind.

But he had other feelings, too. Stretching out one large, callused hand, he laid it upon the enormous bough upon which he sat, and lightly patted the wood. 'Take us someplace... *grand*,' he asked.

The Tree, oblivious, wandered on.

Farther up, Maut Sweetlove's first sign of impending Change came from the squirrels. They, with their red jackets and puffed tails, were a familiar sight up and down the Tree, and by custom they clustered around Maut's eyrie. Her tall figure was often to be seen striding around the woods of Kottow, a bag at her waist filling up with fallen nuts, and come a hard winter, Maut kept the squirrels fed. In return, they brought her trifles they'd discovered in their own foragings. Maut's prize amongst these was a heavy coin, much worn with age and time, of no currency she could spend — but she would not have spent it anyway, for it had taken three strong squirrels working together to haul it up the Tree for her.

She woke that morning to the sound of a clamorous chattering among her smallest friends. Opening her eyes, she found no fewer than eight of them arranged over the patched blankets of her bed, tightly clinging to the bed-clothes. Several more had taken perches about the eyrie: curled up upon the chair Diggory Stokey had made of fallen oak wood; wound into a ball inside the bedding-boxes she had hung from the roof; one inside her own pillow, a fact she discovered when she turned over, eliciting a smothered squeak.

The swaying and juddering began soon afterwards, and prompted a swift and decisive exodus. Half the red squirrels of the Tree streamed away down the trunk; Maut watched it happen, hanging out of her tiny window. Soon she was moved to withdraw inside, for the Tree's motion was profound enough to shake her straight out of the window, were she not careful. Indeed, she had some cares for her eyrie; built to withstand high winds, it had fewer means to bear the regular, rolling motion of the Tree as it strode off yonder.

'Curious,' said she, and ran to open her door, for there came a pounding upon it.

Berengaria Dow stood upon the threshold, clinging to the nearest bough.

'Maut Fey,' she said. '*What* have you done?'

Maut wrinkled her nose at the name. Just because the squirrels were fond of her, they thought her Fey, the Tree-folk, and told her so with the name. Well, and if there *was* a slight curl to the tips of her ears, and a catlike quality about her amber-brown eyes, did that make her fair-folk? No, indeed!

'None of my doing,' she said. 'Look to your own house, and leave me to mine.'

Berengaria was no ill-natured woman as a rule, but unprecedented circumstances produced unprecedented effects; she did not move. 'If it weren't you, who's done it?'

'I should ask the Wizard, if you're stuck on the *why* of it,' retorted Maut. 'Me, I am more interested in the *where.*'

'The Wizard?' gasped Berengaria. 'I can't do that.'

'Well, you won't get any answers from me. I don't know anything.'

Berengaria said nothing; Maut could see the thoughts turning behind her pretty blue eyes. An appealing girl, younger than Maut, not normally with windmills in her head; if she could get a hold on herself, she'd do well enough.

'I will ask the Wizard,' she announced, visibly squaring up to the task. 'If you'll go with me.'

'Not I. I don't go up that high.'

'No more do I, but somebody has to answer for this.'

'Maybe nobody's done it,' suggested Maut. 'Maybe it's just the Tree.'

'But — but then there's no stopping it.'

'Do you want to stop it?'

Berengaria bit her lip. A faint glow of emotion appeared in her sky-coloured eyes.

'Oh, *I* see,' said Maut. 'You've a sweetheart in Kottow.'

'The baker's lad. He's so—'

'The most charming boy alive, no doubt,' interrupted Maut. 'If you're wanting to stay in Kottow, you'd best get off about now. I do believe we are picking up speed.'

'But—' Berengaria sighed. 'But I live *here*.'

'It's your sweetheart or your worldly goods,' said Maut without sympathy. 'Take your pick.'

Berengaria's answer was to direct one long, longing look back in the direction of Kottow. 'Well,' she sighed.

Choice made, Maut thought, and the child had a bit more sense than appeared. 'There's always more baker's lads,' she offered.

'That there are.'

'Happen we'll find a few wherever we are going.'

'Where *do* you think we are going, Maut?'

'Haven't the foggiest.'

Berengaria smiled like the sun. Having abandoned her sweetheart to the past, most of her dismay seemed gone along with him. There was almost a frisking quality to her step as she turned away, and began to venture down the trunk.

'Not seeing the Wizard, then?' Maut called after her.

'I'm going to tell the others!' Berengaria shouted back.

'Tell them what, if you please?'

'That the Tree-witch hasn't a notion!'

Maut closed the door, muttering something to herself.

The possibility of asking the Wizard was not so poor an idea, she thought. After all, the Tree's having the propensity to wander off was no little-known thing; the Elders had been telling those tales for many a year. But it hadn't happened in all that time, and now suddenly it *was*, and Maut for one was curious.

The Wizard, though. No one had seen *him* in many a year, either. Few ventured so high up the Tree, for the air was thin up there, and the clouds so thick you could hardly see where you were putting your feet.

Perhaps there *was* no Wizard, Maut thought. Maybe he'd gone. A singular sort, if not; you wouldn't catch *him* ambling down the Tree to hobnob with his neighbours.

Maut gave a moment's thought to the prospect of climbing so high, and with the whole world rocking like a goodwoman's favourite chair.

No. Not even if she were a squirrel her own self. A body'd have to be out of her wits.

Well, then. If the Wizard had answers, he'd have to bring them to the folk of the Tree himself.

Small likelihood of that.

Most of the folk of the Tree had the sense to live lower down; or at least, not *much* more than halfway up. It was the wind that prompted the choice. All the way up there — miles and *miles* high, some said — it'd tear your house out of the branches and hurl it straight down, you along with it. Nobody built dwellings a ways out from the trunk, up there, and most dwelt elsewhere.

One or two souls were different. Hardier (or perhaps *fool*hardier) than the rest, they lived all the way up, where you could see for thirty miles or more in every direction. They did at least have the sense to tuck themselves right inside the broad, round trunk, in one of the hollow nooks the Tree had (so it seemed) made on purpose for the accommodation of delicate creatures.

One such was Gower Bordekin. Some years ago, Gower had startled the Folk (unflappable types as a rule; they'd have to be, considering their mode of living) by turning up with an arm-chair strapped to his back, tapestry cushions and all. To be fair, he looked like he could easily bear the load, being a hale and hearty sort of man, and not much above forty at the time. He'd been a blacksmith, once, he explained, and had the arms to prove it.

He had also been a travelling merchant and a potion-maker (a fact eliciting a few scoffs).

What he had enjoyed most of all, however, was his wanderings. Gower the Explorer, they called him down below, and on the rare occasions he ventured to descend from his lofty perch, he was always offered a tankard of something good, for he brought splendid tales with him.

Well, and on that very first day of his appearance at the Tree, he had stopped at the bottom of the trunk, and shown no surprise whatsoever upon seeing it; on the contrary, he'd travelled far to reach Kottow. And it was not only the arm-chair he had brought with him.

By sunset, he had hauled the lot up the Tree, through a wily combination of cleverly deployed ropes, and the sheer bodily power that was all his own. He installed himself in a vacant abode (spacious enough, despite the quantity of goods and furniture he thought necessary), and settled down to wait.

'Wait for what?' more than one person had said to him at the time.

Gower Bordekin had only winked and said, 'You'll

11

see.'

Twenty-one years had passed quietly away.

There proved to be more than one curious thing about Gower Bordekin. Another eventually emerged: the years couldn't touch him. They may sail by as plentifully as they pleased, but Gower's hair remained dark, his shoulders unbowed, and his eyes bright. He scrambled up and down the Tree with the same ease as ever, though perhaps he became a little more withdrawn. What he did up there all day, nobody could have said, for few would climb high enough to find out.

On the morning of the Tree's departure, Gower woke some ten minutes before the first tremor, and lay with wide eyes, his heart pounding. After a minute or two passed without event, he cautiously lifted his head, and looked about him.

His house, were it to deserve the name, looked the same as it had last night. There was his dark-oak desk (a more recent addition, with Diggory Stokey's help), all his maps and drawings safely closed away inside. The arm-chair, so well-remembered by the Lower Folk, still stood before it. He had added some engravings to it since that day, though nobody but he could have said what they meant. His clothes-chest sat at the foot of his bed, and the rug of coloured rags maintained its position in the centre of the floor.

Everything but the rug, he'd long ago bolted to the walls.

He rose, throwing his patched blanket aside, and quietly gathered up the rug. This he rolled, and tucked into a small space between the bed and the wall. Everything that was not bolted down, he collected, and tucked into his clothes-chest.

Then he threw open his door and sat upon the threshold, with his legs dangling over the side.

When the tremors came, Gower Bordekin held his breath.

When the *shuddering* and *juddering* started, he began to smile.

And when, with its first, terrific *jolt*, the Tree began to move, Gower Bordekin's voice might perhaps have been heard (by a bird or two, if no one else), raised in a joyous *whoop* of celebration.

CHAPTER TWO

If anyone would know if the Wizard was still up there, Mother Gantry said, it would be Gower Bordekin. As far as the Lower Folk knew — or the Higher, for that matter — nobody lived farther up the boughs than Gower (except, of course, the Wizard himself).

'We must ask him,' said she, for Berengaria's notions had spread fast. 'Ask him if he has seen the Wizard, any time these twenty years. Go on, Diggory.'

'Why must it be me?' Diggory complained.

'My old legs won't take me up there.'

'Aye,' Diggory agreed. 'But why must it be *me*?'

'Why, thou art downright cousinly with the man. Art thou not?'

'I may have carpentered a thing or two for him, in my time,' Diggory allowed. 'But that don't make us bosom companions, Mother.'

Mother Gantry scowled. ''Tis my belief thou'rt afeared.'

'I might be.'

14

'Come, now. Just because the Tree is shaking itself into pieces, *that* need not weigh with a stout heart such as thine.'

Diggory glanced up. Being a kind-hearted man, he had been sitting with Mother Gantry in her kitchen for some time, as the Tree rambled on, though he'd taken up a station at the door — unconsciously echoing that of Gower Bordekin, far above. He did possess a stout heart, as Mother Gantry knew, but he had sense as well.

'I'll go as far as Maut,' he offered.

'The Fey?' Mother Gantry considered this. 'If anybody's to know the doings of a Wizard, I suppose it'd be she.'

'Aye, though she's also nearer to Bordekin than you or I, and accustomed to the heights. Shall I go now?'

'Go,' said Mother Gantry.

Diggory went. He had lived long enough in the Tree to become sure of foot in the heights, and the Tree itself had made the stair-way precisely for this sort of use. Even so, to clamber up it while the thing was jouncing about; that was a mite different. He went slowly, keeping a careful grip upon the boughs, and pausing to be sure of his footing before taking the next step. At such a pace, it took him nearly an hour to climb up to Maut Sweetlove's level.

He found her outside of her house, curled up upon a particularly broad bough with her back set squarely against the trunk. Her eyes grew round as she looked down upon him, making his slow way higher and higher.

'What brings you so high, Diggory?' she called down. 'It's no weather for climbing.'

'Mother Gantry,' he called back.

'Ah.'

'She insisted.' Diggory said no more, saving his breath for the effort of scaling the last several feet. Maut moved over a bit, making space for him upon the bough; he fell into it with a sigh, and sat catching his breath.

'I don't wonder that she is worried,' said Maut after a while.

'She don't like change,' agreed Diggory.

'Few do, all told.'

'Aye, though mayhap it's more than that with her. She's mighty antsy.'

Diggory studied Maut. She looked calm enough, cool as a lake in summer in fact, eating dried chestnuts out of a pocket in her tunic, and watching the scenery go by with placid eyes. A squirrel lay curled in the folds of her skirt, and another perched upon her shoulder, helping itself to bits of her repast.

'You seem untouched,' he remarked.

'Seems to me,' said Maut, without looking at him, 'you don't live in the Tree if you're unwilling to wander.'

'I wonder where we are wandering *to*.'

'Aye, so do I.'

'That's Mother Gantry's thought. She wants to ask the Wizard.'

'So you came to find me?' Maut shook her head. 'As I told Berengaria before now: *I* haven't done this, and I know nothing of the Wizard. And,' she said, fixing him with a stern eye, as he opened his mouth to speak, 'I won't go up high enough to find out.'

'Would you go up high enough to find Bordekin?'

Maut blinked. 'What has Gower Bordekin to do

with this?'

'Maybe nowt. But there's more'n a few things odd about the fellow, you have to admit, and he lives high up, besides. If anybody knows somethin' about the Wizard, it must be he.'

'Send a bird, then,' said Maut. 'You'll not send me.'

'A squirrel?' he offered, smiling at the one asleep in her skirt.

'A word of wisdom from the Fey,' said Maut, a sardonic curl to her lips signalling what she thought of the title. 'Never try to use a squirrel as a messenger. They haven't the brains for it.'

'Well, I don't have a bird.'

'You have your own two feet.'

'Already exhausted from climbin' this far. It's a long way down.'

'That I know.' She sighed, and he sensed a weakening in her resolve. '*Must* it be now?'

'No. Mother Gantry will wait.'

'Not gladly.'

'But she'll wait.' Diggory folded his hands. 'If you don't mind, I'll take a minute or two afore I go back down.'

Maut offered him a cluster of chestnuts. 'Take in the view, while you're here. There is much to see.'

That there was. Kottow lay far behind, long since vanished from sight. Some other town loomed in the near distance, though with its cluster of thatched roof-tops and single church spire, it was another such market town, and of similar character. Diggory saw villages dotted about the landscape beyond, and thickets of woodland cropping up hither and thither, all coming splendidly into leaf. Odd, to witness a flurry of copses from up here; rather like looking down upon a crowd of people, from such a height as to see only the crowns of their heads. A bit lonely, if Diggory were to put a name to the odd feeling he got.

Nothing that he saw stood out as a possible destination for the Tree, if it were possible to guess it. Perhaps the Tree had simply grown bored of Kottow, and would fetch up soon enough on the edge of some other town, or in the midst of one of these many woodlands. Time would tell; Diggory could not.

Maut finished the last of her chestnuts, and brushed the crumbs of nut-husks from her fingers. 'I've been thinking back, to the last time I heard stories of the Wandering-Tree,' she said. 'There's folk still living in Kottow as saw the Tree wander in, or so they used to say. Just turned up one day, spraying earth every which way, and making the ground shake like there was an earthquake going on. Scared the whole town out of their wits, as you might imagine. They all ran away; but they came back the next day, because the Tree stopped not far from the gate, and never moved again.'

'Until today.'

'Until today.' Maut inclined her head.

'How long have you been up here?' Diggory himself was no great veteran of tree life, having joined the folk only a handful of years past.

Maut's answering look had a shifty quality about it. 'A while. Must've been daft in the head to take up such an abode. That's what the Kottow folk said, any road.'

Diggory smiled.

'Perhaps they were right,' Maut added, looking about herself. 'Now look what a fix I'm in.'

Diggory pictured that long-ago day, when a Tree

had taken a fancy to an ordinary market town, and decided to stay a while. 'Was there people living in the Tree back then?'

'When it came into Kottow? Aye, there were. Some of them came down the next day, and went shopping in the town, cool as you please. The folk of Kottow got used to them, soon enough.'

'They're all gone now, I suppose.'

'Must be.'

'Truth be told,' said Diggory, 'if that's to be the end of all this — we fetch up on the edge of some other town, and there we stay — I'll be a mite disappointed.'

'Another town just like Kottow, you mean?' Maut nodded.

'If I wanted to move to another such place, I could walk there meself.'

'Bit of a come-down, to be sure.' Maut shifted, and began to rise (carefully) to her feet, keeping her hands braced against the trunk. 'I'd better be off, if I'm to find Gower.'

She was almost out of earshot before another thought occurred to Diggory. 'Maut!' he shouted. 'Did you ever hear it said where the Tree came in *from*?'

Maut paused, a diminished figure clinging, almost squirrel-like, to the side of the enormous, craggy trunk. She peered down at Diggory, her arrested manner suggesting the thought had only that moment entered *her* head. 'I think not,' she called down. 'I'm sure I would have remembered, if anyone had.'

'Pity,' said Diggory, and began his descent to the relative stability of the Lower Tree, and Mother Gantry's kitchen.

A body'd have to be out of her wits to go scampering up the Tree at *this* of all times, Maut had thought, at no great distance of time. She thought it now, toiling up and around and up and around, as the great boughs groaned and swayed around her, and the Tree plodded ever on. What had she been thinking, to let Diggory Stokey talk her into it?

He had smiled so pleasantly. That was the problem with him. He had such a smiling face: every part of it radiated warmth and mirth and goodness, until you were hard-pressed to say no to him about anything at all. Mother Gantry was a wily one, to use Diggory as her messenger.

Maple leaves gave way to sweet-chestnut, and then to birch and elm all growing together, as Maut slowly ascended. The bark under her hands and feet roughened and turned hard and sharp, then smoothed and went silky, and then put out a profusion of knots and gnarls. Maut had to watch every step she took, and every place she put her hands; she was unused to this part of the Tree. In fact, nothing of it was familiar; you'd think she had never come up so high in her life before.

She paused to catch her breath, and look about herself. She had passed several doorways in the trunk, one or two of whom belonged to people she knew. Up here, though, she was past her knowledge. Whose was the spring-green door with the brass knocker set right in the middle? Or the one a bit farther up, hung with some kind of tapestry, and with a bell fastened off to the left? Neither was Gower's, for certain. Had she then gone too far, and missed his abode altogether? No, surely not. She'd been watching for it so carefully.

Uncertain, she stayed where she was, until her breath evened out and the ache in her feet subsided. So high up was she now, she could no longer distinguish towns or villages far below. The land lay gleaming in the spring sunshine, all mottled, the colours of leaves, old and new. Here and there the deep velvet of fields lay dreaming in the sun; in another part, the sumptuous dark-moss of a forest lay caught up in shadow. She saw clear water, away to the left, stretching out to the horizon.

The Tree showed no signs of slowing down.

'Well,' said Maut aloud. She could climb on forever at this rate, and end up at the Wizard's door after all. *That* was no part of her plan.

Instead, she went up just a little farther, until she drew level with the tapestried door. There, she took hold of the silvery bell, and rang it firmly. A tinkling clarion-sound rang out.

A *creak* sounded almost at once, and a *thunk*, and then the tapestry-curtain was wrenched aside with considerable force. '*Yes?*' said somebody.

Maut had no notion what manner of *somebody* this was. The creature was much shorter than Maut, standing not even four feet high. She had a withered face the colour of milk; a thicket of wispy, silvery hair, in which a quantity of snails resided; eyes like faded chips of amber, presently scowling at Maut with no friendly feeling whatsoever; and garments that looked stitched from leaf-skeletons and old cobwebs, hung here and there with down-feathers and thistle-seeds.

'*What?*' snapped she, when Maut only stared, and said nothing. She held a ladle in her hand, the bowl covered in some gunk of foul appearance, and this she brandished in Maut's face. '*You* of all types ought not to stare so!'

'Sorry,' Maut mumbled, torn between shame at her behaviour and indignation at the response. *She* of all types? Why she? Her hand rose to feel at the curl to the tips of her ears; she forced it back down again. 'I am looking for Gower Bordekin,' she said, collecting her scattered thoughts. 'Is he about here somewhere?'

'Never heard of him.' This closed the conversation, as far as the odd little woman was concerned, for she made to slam the door in Maut's face.

'Wait,' said Maut. 'The Wizard? What of he?'

'What *of* he?'

'Is he — am I near where he lives?'

This elicited a wheezing, cackling laugh. '*He*? Oh, no! You've a long way ahead, if you want to find *him*.'

Maut did not much understand this speech, and said so.

'Get on with you.' One thin but wiry arm shot out to grasp the curtain, and whip it across the doorway. A terrific *slam* followed as the door closed behind it.

Maut sat upon the nearest bough, and thought.

As she sat there, an alteration among the rustling leaves caught her eye, and made itself known to her wandering wits. They were oak again, somehow, though she hadn't thought those grew so far above the base. What's more, they were an odd colour. Tawny-amber, like... well, like gold.

She reached out, and plucked one. It sat heavy in her palm, shining all glossy in the sun.

'Gold leaves,' she said. 'Curious.'

A shout rattled through the door. 'Leave my leaves

alone!' A couple of dull *thuds* suggested a certain ladle had been pounded against it.

Maut tucked her purloined leaf into a pocket in her tunic, and climbed on again.

The next door was some way up, and more commonplace in appearance: a beech-carven thing of uneven planks, doubtless cut from some fallen branch. Maut thumped upon it. 'I'm looking for Gower Bordekin!' she called.

'Farther up!' came the reply.

Maut went farther up, until her arms and legs ached from clinging to the wandering Tree, and her head swam from the dizzying heights she had climbed to. Her relief, then, upon beholding Gower Bordekin himself, sitting in the open doorway of his house with his legs hanging over the side, was profound.

'Gower!' she called. '*Must* you live so high up?'

He beamed, and hollered back: 'Why, it's a delight up here!'

Maut's only response to that was something ill-natured, muttered under her breath where Gower couldn't hear her. She said nothing else for a time, saving her breath for the last of the climb. At length, she sat, blessedly stationary, upon a broad bough near Gower's threshold, and scowled at him.

'Well, Maut Sweetlove,' said Gower, with unimpaired cheer. 'What brings you to my door?'

'You may have noticed,' said Maut sourly, 'that the Tree is on the move.'

Gower's eyes twinkled. 'Might have.'

'*You* look mighty cheery about it.'

'It's of no use to be otherwise,' he pointed out. 'Won't make a scrap of difference, will it now?'

This could not be refuted; Maut did not try. 'I

come up at the behest of Diggory Stokey,' she said, 'who came up at the behest of Mother Gantry, *who*, if you please, would like to ask the Wizard why the Tree has left Kottow, and where it's going.'

'The Wizard?' said Gower quickly. 'I am not he.'

'Nobody thinks you are,' retorted Maut. 'But they do think you've a mighty odd way about you, and if anybody'd know aught about the Wizard, it must be you.'

Gower studied her. 'They said the same sort of things of you, I'll be bound.'

Maut thought of Berengaria, and scowled the more fiercely for it.

'Now you look like Mudleaf,' said Gower. 'Best take the frown off, if I were you.'

'Mudleaf. Is she the bad-tempered body with the ladle?'

'That's she.'

'She *said* she'd never heard of you.'

Gower grinned. 'I might have thieved that ladle, once upon a time. She never forgave me, though I gave it back soon after.'

Maut thought then of the nastiness the said ladle had been caked in, and shuddered. She did not want to know what sort of concoctions Mudleaf liked to brew up. 'Well, but the Wizard,' she persevered. 'Where is he?'

Gower lifted a hand, and pointed a finger. Up.

'Up,' sighed Maut, and shook her head. 'No, I cannot do it. This is as far as I go.'

'Next you'll be asking me to take my part in this intriguing relay,' said Gower. 'Please don't. The Wizard cannot stop the Tree. Nothing can, now; not 'till it chooses.'

'How do you know that?'

Gower only smiled.

'So, it's a climb for nothing,' Maut sighed. 'Diggory shall owe me two or three of Mother's loaves, after this.' She stuck her hand into the pocket in her tunic, and brought out the leaf she had picked not long since. It wasn't gold any longer; only a lacy skeleton of a thing, long dead.

'You may wait with me, for a time,' said Gower. 'Who knows but what you might see something interesting?'

Maut twitched an eyebrow. 'Such as what?'

Gower looked up. A ways above, the Tree's upper boughs grew hazy in Maut's vision, partially obscured by a drifting mist she realised, with a start, was the beginnings of a cloud. Were they so high up as all *that*? 'That's a cloud,' she said, uselessly.

Gower, noticing her expression, shook his head. 'Not really. Not one of the *sky* kind. The Tree makes its own up here, so I've noticed. Or mayhap it's the Wizard.'

Maut watched as thick tendrils of mist coiled slowly around a flourishing thicket of leaves. Up here, they were of a shape and hue she no longer recognised: curling over at the tips into tight little spirals, and all in thunderous sky colours. The branches were less like wood and more like frosted glass.

'What's it want a cloud for?' she ventured.

'The Tree?' said Gower, and shrugged. 'Who knows?'

Maut's fascinated observation of the Tree's cloudish stylings received two interruptions in short order.

The first was the abrupt descent of a small, hard object into her upturned face. It bounced off her cheek, and clattered away down the trunk.

'Acorn,' said Gower.

'It's growing acorns up there?'

Gower shrugged. 'Of a sort.'

'It need not throw them at *me*.'

'You were staring.'

Maut thought, again, of Mudleaf. 'I wasn't staring,' she said. 'I was admiring.'

This promising bout of sophistry ended there, for the second interruption occurred: a marked slowing of the Tree's hitherto steady pace.

'We're... are we stopping?' said Maut, clutching, almost too late, at the bough that bore her, as the Tree gave a sudden shake of its branches.

'Looks like we are,' said Gower. He said nothing more, but Maut, casting a swift glance at his lean face, thought he appeared... puzzled. He was looking all around, as though expecting to see something of note — and, finding nothing, suffering some disappointment.

'I must go down,' said Maut, though her heart sank at the prospect of the long and *long* descent ahead of her. She had yet to stop aching from the climb.

Gower turned his questing gaze upon her, and studied her from head to foot. 'I reckon you're in no shape, yet.'

'I can manage.'

Gower shook his head. 'I've a better thought.'

Five minutes later, Maut made her descent in smooth, graceful fashion, and at no effort whatsoever. Piled into an ingenious contraption of Gower's, a device resembling an oversized basket threaded upon a sturdy rope, she was lowered in easy stages. Gower bore the brunt of it. 'Think nothing of that,' he said easily, his powerful arms bunching as he manipulated the pulley. 'I'm well able to manage.'

That he was, for Maut suffered no inconveniences at all on her way down the trunk — not even a collision with an unluckily-placed bough. Gower had planned his device carefully indeed.

It was only afterwards, once she had reached the ground and got out of the basket, that a curious fact occurred to her. She had assuredly gone down much the same way she had gone up; yet she hadn't seen Mudleaf's curtained doorway in its gold-leafed bower, nor the spring-green door with the big, brass knocker that came below.

Well, she was distracted, that was all, and had missed them.

After all, the Tree had stopped.

CHAPTER THREE

Diggory Stokey was among the first to get down from the Tree, upon its coming to a halt. It had wandered for nearly the whole day, and evening would soon be drawing in. There would not be much time to explore the Tree's new choice of home — if it was such. They had fetched up on the edge of a forest, shadowed at this hour, its evergreen trees growing thickly, and close together. An expanse of scrubby grass bordered its edge, much grown over with cow-parsley and nettles. Wending its way through the verdure ran a thin track, the sort made by the regular passage of human feet — and carts, too, perhaps, for either side of the track the grass was sparser, and flattened.

'Mayhap we won't be stoppin' for long,' Diggory warned, as Mother Gantry, Berengaria Dow, Maut Sweetlove and others joined him below. 'Look.' He pointed at the nearest of the Tree's tangle of roots, each one thicker around than his own arms. 'They aren't goin' down again.'

Were the Tree planning to remain, Diggory

thought, it would surely be stabilising itself; sending its roots back down into the deep earth, where they would stay for many years to come. It had not done so. Many roots remained above the surface, poised, ready to jump into motion again at any moment.

Mother Gantry took in all this with a suspicious eye. 'Right,' she said. 'Up we go again.' She succeeded in hustling Berengaria away, and some few others, despite their protests — 'The Tree won't wait for *thee*, Tib Brackenbury!' — but Maut came to where Diggory stood near the broad base of the trunk, and joined him in staring out into the gathering twilight.

'Why's it stopped, if not to stay?' she said, in a hushed way.

'Seems it may be waitin' for sommat.'

Maut nodded, and folded her arms. 'Right.'

'Or some*one*,' Diggory added a moment later. 'See there.'

A light approached. Held some way off the ground, Diggory judged, and steady enough; not a lone wanderer, then. Soon his ears picked up the sounds of large wheels turning, and the soft *thud, thud* of hooves upon earth. No chatter, though. The folk in the farm-cart, or whatever it was, were the quiet sort.

The cart drew up, and stopped near the Tree. Not a large one, all told: only a single horse drew it, one of the brawny cob types favoured by farmers, and the wagon behind was a rude affair, with few graces about it. Three people were in it: one driving (a stout man, his features obscured beneath the wide brim of his hat); and two others seated in the wagon, neither of whom Diggory could clearly see, for they were shrouded in travelling-cloaks, and did not immediately look up. The light he had seen came from a lanthorn — two of them, in fact, hanging either side of the driver.

'Ahoy, there,' Diggory called. 'Are you come a-lookin' for the Tree?'

'Aye,' said the driver.

One of his passengers got down from the wagon, but only one. This newcomer approached Diggory and Maut, pushing back the hood of her woollen cloak. The garment, to Diggory's eye, had the unlovely sturdiness favoured by a practical nature and a scant purse. The woman herself seemed somewhat more out of the ordinary: a little older than he and Maut, though not too much, with a pale face and a fall of deep-red hair pulled back in a loose knot. She smiled upon them both.

'I thought I was going to miss it,' said she, looking up at the Tree. 'One ought not to be surprised at how fast a Tree can move, I suppose, when it has a mind to.'

'How did you know it would be here at all?' Maut said.

'I Saw it,' she said, without seeming disposed to explain this mystifying statement. 'There is room for me, I hope?'

'There's always room,' said Diggory, all smiling welcome. 'The Tree's canny that way.'

The lady — for lady she was, by her speech and manner, despite the plainness of her attire — made them a graceful bow. 'I shall be honoured if you'll accept me into your fellowship. I have waited a long time for an opportunity like this.'

'*Have* we a Fellowship, Diggory?' said Maut, in her humorous way.

'Sommat like that. Here, m'lady, we'll find you a berth.'

'My name is Ysabelon,' said the lady.

And what a musical name it was, to be sure. Diggory gazed upon the lady, all bemusement, for he'd never encountered such as she. He cleared his throat. 'Ah — the accommodations likely ain't what you're used to,' he apologised.

Ysabelon looked down at her thick cloak, all mud-spattered about the hem, and her worn and scuffed shoes beneath. 'And what do you suppose I am used to?' she said, looking up at him again, and with a merry twinkle in her eye.

Maut cuffed him (lightly). 'It's my belief we ought to hurry,' she said. 'The Tree likely won't wait for long.'

Ysabelon nodded, and permitted herself to be assisted up into the boughs. She had little luggage with her, only a traveller's pack, such as peddlers used. Diggory took charge of this, receiving a gracious smile and a thank-you as reward. The cart which had conveyed her to the Tree had turned and gone before they had even got as far up as Mother Gantry's door.

Mother herself stood framed in the doorway, eyeing Ysabelon with open suspicion. 'And what might this be?'

'Our new neighbour, Mother,' said Diggory firmly. 'She's come a long way to join us, so you be good to her, aye?'

'Come a long way?' repeated Mother in disbelief. 'And I thought thee a man of sense, Diggory Stokey.'

'It is true,' said Ysabelon mildly. 'It may seem strange, but I assure you I have not come here to cause any trouble for you.'

31

Maut's lips twitched, but it was Mother Gantry who said what they were all thinking. 'Hard to see how anyone could cause *more* trouble than we've got,' and as if to punctuate this statement, the Tree gave a great shiver, and set off walking again.

A lucky catch saved Ysabelon from being tumbled straight out of the Tree. 'Mind how you go,' said Diggory, quickly releasing the lady, the moment he was certain she was stable.

'We'd better get thee settled,' said Mother Gantry.

Ysabelon took a long look up into the boughs, where several of the Tree's residents sat curiously taking in her arrival. Diggory realised her return stare was no idle scrutiny: she studied each face in turn. 'If there is a tall man here,' said she, 'older than me, with dark hair and arms like this—' and here she made a gesture about her own, indicating sizeable musculature — 'I would be glad to have speech with him.'

'The blacksmith?' said Maut. 'You're known to each other, are you?'

'Somewhat,' murmured Ysabelon.

Diggory and Maut exchanged a look. How could Ysabelon and Gower Bordekin have met before? Gower had barely left the Tree in twenty years; everyone knew that. And Mother Gantry had given no sign of recognising Ysabelon, either, so the lady had never come to the Tree before.

'That is, he is familiar to me,' said Ysabelon. 'I may not be so to him.'

Maut's face said, clearly enough, that she gave up the point: life had become a sequence of mysteries, and she would not bother herself overmuch about this one.

Diggory, though, felt a curiosity to know more. When Mother Gantry had chosen an empty abode for Ysabelon's use, and rustled up a quantity of spare household goods to kit it out, Diggory volunteered himself to escort her up there, and settle her in.

Absorbed in this, he did not see Maut Sweetlove settling herself back into Gower Bordekin's basket-lift, and — with a peremptory tug upon the rope — ascending slowly back up into the distant boughs.

'If you don't mind my askin', milady,' said Diggory, hovering upon the threshold of Ysabelon's new dwelling with her peddler's pack in his hands, 'What did you mean, when you said you'd Seen the Tree?'

She, engaged in a survey of her new space, did not immediately reply. Mother Gantry had surprised Diggory when she had said: 'There's an empty spot just above that should suit thee nicely, Mistress Ysabelon. Right inside the trunk, with a good door. Diggory will take thee up.' This came as news to him: not because Mother had presumed him willing to act as guide (for he was), but because he had not known there to be any space at all inside the trunk. Not this close to the ground. Such dwellings were always the most popular with the residents, and he had not heard that anybody had lately left.

'Gadzooks, Mother, don't tell me we've left someone behind?' he'd said, aghast.

'No, no,' said Mother Gantry, and Diggory was almost sure that she winked at him.

'Then how comes it that there is room?' said he.

'The Tree contrives,' was all she would say on the subject, though she did add, with a roll of her eyes, 'Thou ought to know *that*, by now.'

He had been living in the Lower Boughs for some years, this was true. But it was Mother who usually found space for those as came to join them, and he had never given it any previous thought as to how.

So he shrugged, and took the lady a ways upwards, as Mother directed. And as she had said, there was a suitable house there, between his own and that of Tib Brackenbury above. The door — stout and sound, as promised — stood open in welcome. Diggory wondered who had opened it, and then dismissed the thought. Foolish to ask such questions.

'I Dreamed it,' answered the lady Ysabelon at last, having given a satisfied nod to her surroundings. Hers was a spacious enough plot, the walls nicely smoothed, and with a tiny, round window admitting light and air from the outdoors. Already it had a bed, which unless Diggory missed his guess was growing out of the wall. Blankets of moss and heather covered it, and spilled some way over the floor.

'Dreamed,' he repeated, and smiled. 'Your dreams are a sight more useful'n mine, then.'

'Sometimes. I am as prone to useless, disturbing dreams as anybody else, I suppose, but once in a while…' She removed her cloak, and looked about for somewhere to hang it.

'I can fix you up with a hook—' he began, eager to help. But as he spoke, a peg emerged from the wall next to the door, with an audible *pop*.

'Thank you,' said Ysabelon, perhaps to him, or perhaps to the Tree, and hung up her cloak. Beneath it she wore a simple gown of red cloth with a blue girdle. Nothing of this attire was sumptuous, but she wore it with the grace of a queen. Diggory, in his plain brown doublet and patched hose, felt a peasant beside her.

'And—' he said, attempting, without descending into rudeness, to return to his earlier subject, '—and having Dreamed about the Tree, what brought you to enter it?'

She glanced at him, a keen look, as though she might by this means be able to see into his mind, and understand his thoughts. Well, and if she could Dream up visions of future happenings, and they'd come true, perhaps she could. 'I would like to go wherever it is going,' she said. 'I don't yet know where that might be, but I *feel* that I ought to go too.'

And on this point she would not be drawn further, despite Diggory's questions. 'Your tall blacksmith, then?' he said, abandoning a fruitless line of enquiry. 'Did you Dream him up, too?'

'Something like that,' said she. 'He *is* here, isn't he?'

'Said to be,' said Diggory. 'I cannot rightly promise it. The Tree's been shaking about a lot lately. He might have fallen out.'

He jested, but there was a sour note beneath which surprised and displeased even his own self. What, was he feeling jealous over a stranger's interest in Bordekin? She might be a comely woman and every bit of a lady, but he had no cause for *that*.

'Not him,' said Ysabelon. 'If he is up in the heights, then I must go up there too.'

'Not tonight, at least,' begged Diggory. 'It ain't safe to climb so high at any time, just now, but especially not at night.'

Ysabelon agreed to this, much to his relief, and produced a yawn. 'I am rather tired,' she admitted. 'I have travelled for three days and nights with scarcely a pause for rest.'

'You were mighty eager to reach us in time, then,' said Diggory.

'Yes,' said the lady. 'I was.'

At that moment, Maut was clambering out of Gower Bordekin's giant basket again, and alighting upon the bough beside his home.

'There's a lady below,' she told him, as he secured the woven lifting-contraption, and stretched out his weary arms. 'Just got on. She's looking for you.'

'A lady I know?' he said, his brows rising.

'A lady as knows you. Maybe not the other way about. She's right comely.'

Gower looked mystified.

'She's not the sort we usually get,' said Maut, taking a seat, and looking out over the land. The sun was just vanishing beneath the horizon, but the moon had not yet risen, and few lights shone below. 'A real lady, with fancy speech and the lot.' She smiled faintly, and added, 'Diggory is mighty taken with her.'

Gower Bordekin considered this news. 'She hasn't said why she's boarded the Tree, I suppose?'

Maut shook her head. 'Oh, no. This lady's as mysterious as ever you could be. But she was glad to catch up with us. Gone to some lengths to do so, I'd wager.'

'Hm,' said Gower. 'I'll go below.'

'Now?' said Maut. 'I can't equal your trick with the basket, I'm sorry. I haven't the muscles to match you.'

'Not now. Tomorrow.'

Maut felt a touch upon her beskirted leg, and looked down to find a squirrel there, paws held up to catch the morsels she must surely have about her somewhere.

She did, of course, and some of these she distributed now. The squirrel accepted three chunks of dried chestnuts, and set about gobbling them down.

'Where do you think we are going, Gower?' said Maut after a while. 'It seems to me you know more about it than the rest of us.'

'Oh?' said Gower. 'Why do you think so?'

'The rest of us, we're... puzzled. Stumped, even, and perhaps a bit afraid.'

'*You* were never afraid of anything in your life, Maut Fey,' interrupted Gower. 'You cannot claim otherwise; I wouldn't believe you.'

She smiled. 'I've known fear, but it isn't today,' she acknowledged. 'Some of us feels differently there, but not you. You aren't afeared, and you aren't confused. If I had to guess, I'd say as you are enjoying this.' She directed a stern look at him, halting him in the act of lighting the great iron-wrought lanthorn that hung by his door (a creation of his own hands, she'd be bound).

'Why, I am,' said Gower, with one of his big smiles.

'Indeed. What's more, you've been awaiting it. Have not you?'

'I don't deny it.' Gower turned back to his lanthorn, and coaxed a flame alight.

'Well, then: why? What do you know about where we're off to?'

Gower paused, perhaps to arrange his thoughts. He did not look at Maut; his gaze was fixed someplace else, inside his own mind belike. 'I know nothing for sure,' he said at last. 'But I've an idea.'

'And what's that.'

'I think we are not going *to* someplace as much as we are going *back to* somewhere.'

Maut nodded slowly. 'I believe I see what you mean.'

'This Tree is not like other trees,' he said.

'You don't say.'

His smile returned, briefly. 'It was born of no Tree that *we* know. It grew from no seed; leastwise, not the kind you can find in these parts. Wherever it came from, then, it isn't from around here.'

Maud nodded. 'You think it is going back to wherever it came from.'

'That's what I believe.' Gower nodded.

'And where is that?'

Gower shrugged his massive shoulders. 'A place where Trees like this are not so uncommon. Well, now. Who wouldn't want to go there?'

Maut grinned, as a flicker of excitement sprang to life somewhere within. 'When you put it like that, Gower Bordekin... I believe I am going to enjoy this, too.'

CHAPTER FOUR

It did not suit Gower Bordekin to have speech with the mysterious lady newcomer. To be Seen in a dream, and one that was not of his own making, must make anybody uneasy, so he thought. It certainly made *him* so. Maut Sweetlove was right to call him enigmatic. He had his secrets, and he had every intention of keeping them — at least for the time being.

So, early the following morning, before anybody was yet likely to be rising from their beds, Gower set forth from his own, snug house, and began an ascent into the mists that swirled above.

The Tree had gone on all night, as near as anybody could tell. It had by now settled into a steady gait, with less of the shakings and swayings about, much to the relief of those inside. It had not stopped again, nor even slowed down. It went on at a solid, ground-eating pace that suggested it had yet some way to go.

Gower paused only briefly to look about. Last night, they had been approaching the kind of expansive, deep and dark forest that proposed to go on forever. They were now travelling along the edge of it; had been all night, most likely. There being little to see out there, he turned his eyes upwards, and climbed.

Mist soon swallowed him. It had an odd scent about it, something crisp and sharp. So thick was it, he could see only a foot or so ahead, and had to take especial care where he put his hands and feet. Nonetheless, he climbed. Had he been entirely honest with Maut, he might have mentioned that this ascent was not altogether unfamiliar to him. He had done it before. He always came down again with a thick head and his thoughts wandering in the oddest way, so he did not often make the ascent; once in a great while, no more.

There were no other houses above Gower's. Never had been, as far as he could tell. The trunk narrowed sharply once a person entered the mists, leaving no room for a dwelling. And nobody could be strange enough to put a house out on the thinning boughs up there, with a cloud all around. Talk, then, of a Wizard hidden somewhere above was nonsense. There was no Wizard.

Save, perhaps, for Gower himself.

Right at the apex of the Tree, where the branches grew too thin to climb any higher, the mist was thickest of all. Here Gower stopped, and sat, and bethought himself of what he meant to do. He breathed deeply, letting the mist fill his lungs, and as he sat there the world changed around him. As it always did.

He saw visions in that mist, all the brighter and more vividly the longer he sat and breathed. Perhaps the lady newcomer Saw similarly, when she slept; sometime, when his secrets weighed less heavily upon him, he might like to question her about it. For now, he only wanted to Look.

He rarely performed this ritual, anymore. It tired him, for no reason he understood, and rarely proved fruitful. He Saw plenty, but nothing that could make any sense, for the pictures in the mist were disjointed and unclear, and he recognised so few of the faces that he saw.

So it proved again. Blurred scenes formed in the mist, rushed through a torrent of activity he knew not how to decipher, and faded again. He Saw only two things that were familiar to him: the Tree itself, and his own face.

The Tree was a-wander, there in the dreaming mists, as it had always been. More than twenty years had passed since he had first come up this high, and seen the visions here, but even that very first time, the vision-Tree had appeared in motion. He had known the day was coming when the real one would do so in truth.

Where, though, was it going? That he could not determine, even now. He only knew that he himself would be important, somehow, whenever it got there.

Perhaps the lady had Seen the same thing.

Try as he might, straining his eyes and his hopes as he sorted through every wisp and flicker of Seeings, he could find no new insights there. Nothing in the visions had changed. As far as the Mists knew — or would consent to tell — the Tree might be going anywhere at all.

He gave a sigh, and sat for a time, no longer scrutinising those elusive Mists but descending instead into his own thoughts. Twenty-one years: so long a time to wait. So long a time to *hope*. Had it been in vain? He had sought to learn the answer to that question this morning; instead, he would have to wait again. Wait, and wait, and wait.

He rose from his seat, ready to retrace his steps, and return to his own abode below. But as he grasped a pair of branches in readiness for the descent, he paused, feeling something altered under his hands.

The Tree rarely evinced any manner of feeling or thought. He knew this thoroughly, having often attempted to discern just such a thing in the living wood around him. He never had, or almost never, the Tree having been deep, deep in slumber since long before he had arrived. But here, at *last*, he encountered a change.

A flicker of warmth under his hands. Not the warmth of a fire on a cold day, or the sun on a hot one. More a warmth of feeling; an intangible sensation, suggestive of — of — anticipation. Joy.

Wherever the Tree might be going, she was wild with excitement to get there.

'The Tree stopped for you,' said Diggory Stokey later that day, having sought out the lady Ysabelon in her new abode.

'Did it?' said she, rather vaguely, being engaged in darning a hole in one of her gowns.

'I believe so.' Diggory sat near the door, feeling too plain a crow to invade the lady's space too far. 'It is the only time we have stopped since the Tree began to walk, and it stopped only long enough for you to join us.'

'She,' said Ysabelon, without looking up.

Diggory blinked. 'What's that?'

'She,' said Ysabelon again. 'Your Tree is no *it*, but a she.'

Silent in wonder, Diggory said nothing.

Ysabelon looked up at him. 'What, has this never crossed your mind before?'

'That the Tree might be a person, just such as you or I?' Diggory thought about that. 'Somewhat, mayhap. It — *she* — has been known to help us out, once in a while. Such as — well — *she* once caught Aggie Notekyn's child, when the babe all but fell out. Some say as it was chance only, but I think not. A branch *moved*, I would swear to it, and got in the way just in time to catch the child. And not a mite of harm done, neither, for it was all over soft leaves.'

Ysabelon smiled. 'You see?'

'And she has made space for you,' Diggory added. 'As anyone'd tell you, this room here is new since yesterday. Used to be, Tib Brackenbury's house sat right atop Mother Gantry's, and now there is this.'

Ysabelon grew thoughtful, and returned to darning her gown.

'The Tree finds *you* special in some fashion,' Diggory persisted. 'And the same is true the other way about, I would wager, for here you are, after your three days an' nights of travellin' to get here.'

Ysabelon appeared absorbed in her sewing.

'Will you not tell me what you're about?' said Diggory softly. 'Folk are mighty uncertain just now, and would take well to a spot of insight.'

'The thing is,' said Ysabelon, setting down her needle. 'I don't know anything. Not for certain. I only Saw — the Tree, walking, just as it is now. I felt where it would be, and at what time, and I *knew* — though I don't know how — that I ought to be on it.'

Diggory nodded, and waited for more.

But Ysabelon shrugged. 'I have nothing more to tell you, Mr. Stokey. Save that I Saw your Gower Bordekin already here, and knew *him* to be important somehow, too.'

Diggory sighed, a mite wistfully, perhaps wishing that it might have been *he* who was of some importance to the lady.

'You haven't Seen where we are going?' he persevered. 'Not even last night, while you were sleeping in the Tree itself?'

Ysabelon shook her head. She seemed to hesitate, as though on the point of saying something else. But she eyed Diggory uncertainly, and after some moments, closed her lips again, and sat in silence with her sewing.

Diggory rose from the three-legged stool upon which he had seated his bulk. 'Gower won't come down,' he said. 'He never does.'

Ysabelon nodded once. 'Then I must go up.' This was said decisively, and attended by a resolute laying-aside of the mending, as though she proposed to journey to the top of the Tree without further loss of time.

But she had not done more than advance upon the doorway — while Diggory, with all due haste, moved himself out of the way of it — before something happened to drive all thought of Gower Bordekin out of her head.

The Tree stopped again. Abruptly, with a jerk; and this was no restful pause, for it held itself still with a palpable tension, and a faint tremor through the trunk. Poised, Diggory thought, on the brink of something.

Ysabelon met Diggory's gaze, her own eyes rather wide. 'Has she done this before?'

Diggory only shook his head. Any words he might have uttered were lost, for in the next instant, the Tree surged into motion again with a great *leap*, and began to run.

Clinging to the doorframe for fear of being dashed into the boughs, Diggory bethought himself of prayer, and spake something jumbled, under his breath.

He could not precisely have described what happened next. There came no flash of light, nor clap of thunder; no impact, no tangible sensation whatsoever. Nonetheless, Diggory *felt* something; some change in the air, some shift in the light. A scent, a sound, a feeling — all of these, or none. He only knew that everything — *everything* — had, all of a sudden, changed.

The Tree's reckless pace slowed to a weary amble.

And then, at last, she slowed and stopped. A great gust of wind rustled through her ancient boughs, setting the leaves a-shiver; and with this evocative *sigh*, she settled at last.

'We're stopped,' said Diggory, foolishly.

Ysabelon permitted this fatuous observation to pass. She had gone to the door, and now stood looking out of it, with her hands braced against the frame. 'Do you recognise this, Mr. Stokey?'

Diggory joined her at the threshold, and looked his fill.

Surrounding them was... forest. Still the forest, he thought, and felt a pang of disappointment together with puzzlement. He would have sworn that something profound had happened; that they had taken a single step (in the Tree's own, odd fashion), and travelled, somehow, an inordinately long way in the process. Had he imagined it all?

But a moment's reflection saw the error of this thinking. 'This ain't the same forest,' he said.

Mutely, Ysabelon shook her head.

The forest along whose edges they had travelled overnight was composed of knotted old evergreen trees: gnarly yews and fresh-scented pines, and others to which Diggory could put no name. The air had been crisp and chill, and smelling of pine-sap and loam.

This forest was altogether Other. An expanse of forest-floor met his eyes, all soft earth covered over with wild-weeds and clambering vines. Here and there rose a mighty tree, its trunk almost as wide in girth as that of the Kottow Tree. Glancing up, Diggory suffered a moment's vertigo, for they rose and *rose*, so high he could barely grasp the age of them. Ancients, all, in this distant forest, and the air held a spellbound, muted quality to it, as though no one had set foot under these glorious old trees for many ages of man.

Perhaps they hadn't.

'Do you know this place?' said Diggory, in a half-whisper, for it somehow seemed uncouth to make a loud noise in so still and beautiful a place.

Ysabelon shook her head, more in wonder than negation. 'I may have Seen a bit of it, here and there in a Dream. I feel that, distantly, I remember…'

The Tree appeared settled indeed, though perhaps not forever, for many a grand, mighty root had not yet gone down into the earth. Perhaps they might, in time, or perhaps the Tree proposed to wander on a-ways yet.

But that she had no such intention for now, Diggory felt certain, for she was still, wholly still, for the first time in days.

A lean shape fell past his vision, on its way down to the ground: Tib Brackenbury.

'Tib!' Diggory called.

The wiry little man looked up. 'Hurry up, Diggory!' said he. 'Or shall you linger with the lady, while the rest of us looks about ourselves?' He punctuated this suggestive statement with a wink, and then turned his attention from Diggory, as he strode off towards the nearest of the grand old trees.

'I wonder,' said Diggory, 'if all these trees are like ours?'

Ysabelon had gone back inside, to fetch her cloak and her boots. 'Shall we follow Mr. Brackenbury's example, and find out?'

'Aye,' said Diggory, a boy's grin wreathing his face. He went off to gather his own warmer garments, whistling through his teeth, a thing he had not done (though the fact hadn't occurred to him) in many a year.

PART TWO
THE LOST FOREST

CHAPTER ONE

Mudleaf had no intention of haring off madly into the depths of a mysterious forest, like the rest of the lummocks below. She had too much sense. One might even term it wisdom; the deep wisdom of a far-sighted creature, older by far than the children that had colonised the Kottow Tree, and wily.

Lost Forests tended to be forgotten for good reason, thought she, and this one had all the marks of a forest thoroughly lost. Why, everything in it was sound asleep! The hush to the air told her that much. Not so much as a bird stirring.

She watched from her vantage high up in the Tree. The fools got down without a second thought, and streamed away into the woods, equipped with little more than a cloak and a stout pair of boots. What they thought to accomplish out there, with nothing useful to hand, Mudleaf couldn't have said. Nothing much.

When Mudleaf was ready to venture down, she made sure to take her ladle with her.

But she had not gone far before a voice stopped her: a low, mild one, belonging to the man Gower.

'Even the wary Mudleaf is to go down! My, my.'

He was on his way down, too, or so it seemed, for he had on a shabby old coat made of sheepskin, or some such, and thick boots. He at least had the sense to carry aught else with him: a half-length staff of doughty oak wood was strapped to his back, and the handle of a knife stuck out of the top of one boot.

'We aren't here at random,' said Mudleaf defensively. 'Something has brought us. Why shouldn't I find out what it is, same as the rest of you?'

'No reason in the world,' said Gower easily. He nodded at the door below Mudleaf's: spring-green, and with a brass knocker in the middle. 'And Wildboots?'

Mudleaf had been going to pass Willow Wildboots' door without knocking, being of an unsociable disposition herself. She said this.

'Come, there are sure to be dangers abroad,' said Gower, nodding in the direction of the vast expanse of forest before him. 'Now's no time to be shy.'

'*Shy*, do you call it?' growled Mudleaf. But, being unable to deny the essential justice of his rebuke, she stormed up to the little green door, and pounded a fist against it.

It opened instantly.

'Yes?' said Willow, already kitted out for adventuring, in a leather jerkin and britches, and a hardy leaf-woven coat. Upon seeing who assailed his door, his smile disappeared. 'Mudleaf?'

'Willow.' The word said sourly, and with a glower. 'Are you going down?'

'Any moment!' said Willow, with that irritating earnestness he had, and disappeared briefly into his house. He emerged a moment later, carrying a small club, which he attached to a loop upon his belt. Then, sweeping back his mop of earth-coloured hair, in which strings of twigs and acorns clacked, he squared his shoulders and said: 'On we go!'

Mudleaf regarded him sourly. He was no impressive specimen, being slightly shorter than she, and spindly of limb, though she supposed there must be some wiry strength there. He was a young fool, that was the trouble with him; reckless and thoughtless. Bound to be.

Gower was right: he couldn't be permitted to wander around out there alone. Who knew what manner of ruckus he would kick up, if left to himself?

So she took no issue with that "we", instead continuing her slow and steady passage down the Tree. Gower went ahead of her, Willow came behind.

The process took some time.

When at last the unlikely trio arrived at the bottom, they found another of the Tree's residents still lingering there. Mudleaf recognised the fool woman who had knocked upon her door not long ago, only to ask a lot of nonsensical questions.

'Maut?' said Gower. 'I thought you'd have been gone already.'

'I wondered if you'd be coming down.' She smiled at him, but distractedly.

Gathered around her feet were twenty or thirty squirrels. Some of them came from the Tree, Mudleaf supposed, being the red-suited kind she often saw. But there were others there, black-furred or white, no sort of squirrel she had ever seen before.

51

Maut was feeding them.

'Already?' said Gower, watching this display with an expression of bemusement.

Maut merely shrugged. Her gestures said, without need of words, 'Dunnot ask me, I don't know.'

'You'll be staying here with your entourage?' said Gower.

For some reason, Maut looked at Mudleaf.

Mudleaf glared back.

'I think not,' said Maut, turning away with the faintest of smiles. 'They have full enough bellies for now, and won't mind my taking a turn elsewhere.' Glancing at Gower, she added, 'Have you a notion where to go?'

Gower's brows rose. 'Why ask me?'

'You've more idea what's afoot than the rest of us, that I knew since the start,' said Maut. 'Except, perhaps, the newcomer.'

Gower looked about, a little wildly, as though expecting to see the lady jump out from behind a tree. 'And where is she?'

'Gone off already. With Diggory, and Mother Gantry.'

'Mother's off out?' This news clearly surprised the man.

'Said the others'd get up to no end of trouble without her along to keep them in order.' Maut found this amusing, for she chuckled as she spoke.

Mudleaf drew herself up, a stinging retort upon her lips. Some folks needed an older and wiser head about, to knock some sense into them! That was how it went, with some people.

But this rebuke went unspoken, for she noticed at that moment that Willow Wildboots was gone.

'We've lost one already,' said Mudleaf, interrupting some idle remark of Gower's.

Maut looked up sharply. 'Lost?'

'Wildboots,' said Gower, glancing about frowningly. 'I didn't see where he went.'

'Nor I,' said Maut.

Mudleaf, seeing that they were a useless pair, without a pertinent thought between the two of them, set off. Willow might have snuck away soundlessly enough to avoid notice, but he had left a print or two, and these she followed. They led around the wide trunk of the Kottow Tree, and revealed young Wildboots standing on the other side of it, gazing up.

'I saw something fly into the branches,' said he, as Mudleaf joined him.

'A bird, belike,' said Mudleaf, unimpressed.

Willow Wildboots nodded his head several times. 'Aye! A bird!'

'So, then? What's that matter?'

'Twas an odd bird,' said Willow, still searching for a further glimpse of the thing. 'All over colours, and with a long tail.' He made a swooping gesture with his small hands, indicative of a sweepy length of plumage.

'Nonsense,' said Mudleaf. 'There aren't such things.'

'There's one,' said Willow. 'And it's living in our Tree. Look, there goes another.'

Mudleaf permitted herself a sigh, but she looked up.

And there was. A gigantic birdy-thing, or so it seemed, with a great long curvy neck and more feathers than a bird ought to know what to do with, most of them tail. The creature was the colour of roses and sky; its tail shone with a dawny sunshine; and it sang a fluting song as it flew, the kind to warm a heart even as wizened as Mudleaf's.

'See,' said Willow, when Mudleaf didn't speak. 'I told you.'

Mudleaf merely nodded, finding her words. 'Summer save us,' she said at last. 'What manner of forest is this?'

'Enchanted,' said Willow, stoutly, and with authority. 'Must be. How else does a bird come to look like that?'

Mudleaf looked wildly about, in much the way the man Gower had, when reminded of the lady. 'Sure to be more,' she said.

Willow, energised by the mere thought, showed signs of setting off at once into the undergrowth.

'Wait,' said Mudleaf, and grabbed his shoulder. 'They aren't all like to be pretty. Some may be dangerous. You listen to your elders, Willow Wildboots, and don't go haring off like the rest of them fools.'

Willow paused, impatient, and shrugged free of her grip. 'Doubtless you're right,' said he. 'But what else are we to do? If you want to sit at home and cook soup while the rest of us adventures, that's your business, but it won't do for me.'

Mudleaf hid her ladle behind her back. 'It'd be safer,' she offered.

Willow treated this with the scorn it deserved. 'And yet you're here,' he pointed out. 'You came down, too. Why then, if you won't do owt of interest?'

Mudleaf hesitated. What had she planned to do, at that? She felt like two Mudleafs stuck in the one head:

54

one cautious-like, and wary of the depths of a lost forest such as this. One as eager to explore as the rest of the fools, no more willing to hide away than they were.

'We go,' she decided, 'but not beyond sight of our Tree. How's that?'

Willow looked up and up, all the way up the tall, tall trunk of the Kottow Tree, doubtless figuring in his fool of a head how far around it could be seen. 'It'll do to start,' he decided. 'I'll be leading.'

'Not you!' snapped Mudleaf. 'Rash young head that you've got, I'll not follow your lead.'

'Then you'll stay here and make soup,' said Willow, not fooled by the hiding of the ladle behind Mudleaf's back. 'I will bring you back a feather or whatnot from yonder beasties,' and he pointed up, to where the parti-coloured birds had gone.

Mudleaf glowered. 'Don't blame me if you gets yourself broken to bits. I'll not wade in to save you.'

Willow grinned, and without another word, darted away. Muttering invective under her breath, Mudleaf dashed off in pursuit.

Behind them, Gower and Maut had gone away too, apparently unconcerned for the fate of the Tree's smaller folk. Anyone who'd taken a look at Mudleaf before could hardly blame them: tough as the Tree's own roots, was she, and maybe as old, too. Willow might be another matter.

On they went for a time, senses alert, eyes everywhere, but without much effect, for naught happened. At least at first. They passed a grand old tree or two, wide around at the base, and too tall to see the heights of. Oak, belike, thought Mudleaf, for the ridges and hue of the bark suggested such. But the fallen leaves littered about the ground were not those of the oak, in fact, nor of any tree she recognised. They were larger, much larger; some were bigger than her own head. Green enough, though, in an oakish way — though, wait a moment, they were not. They were, and then they were not, for that one just there was as blue as a winter sky, and the next the colour of heather-bloom, and another yellow like the buttercup—

She blinked, and took another look, and they were all green again.

'Willow,' said she. 'I believe my eyes are playing tricks upon me.'

He stopped, halfway around the gnarly bole of yet another ancient, and grinned back at her. 'See, you've need of a young pair of eyes. Mine are sound enough.'

'So everything is green?'

His brows went up. 'Green? Why, no. Everything but, more like.'

Mudleaf was silent with horror.

'See, this,' said Willow, stooping to collect some two or three fallen leaves. He held one up: the size of a dinner-plate, with a point to the tip, and incidentally as bright-red as a fresh cherry — no, the dull green of a pine-needle — no, cherries.

Mudleaf's head began to spin.

'Glamours,' whispered she. 'But which is the true vision?'

Willow looked confused.

'I'm seeing two different places,' Mudleaf explained. 'One's homely enough, not so different from the forests at home, though everything may be giant-sized. And the other's all parti-coloured like my Mam's skirts, and like a forest has no business being

56

at all.'

'I like the colours,' said Willow, fatuously, and smiled at the cherry-red leaf. 'What else, for woods as is home to the likes of them birds?'

'Godlings save us, is everything a mad hue about here?' Mudleaf blinked and blinked again, and the more she did so, the more her vision shifted. The greenery lessened, and the colours grew, and finally there wasn't a familiar thing to be seen anywhere.

'Enchanted forests,' she spat. 'Bah. Like it's been raining magic this long age through.'

'Raining magic,' said Willow, looking up at the skies, and a stray droplet of lingering rain splashed upon his cheek. 'Perhaps it has.'

Diggory Stokey attended the lady Ysabelon, though he'd swear it was more her idea than his.
Being as she was housed so near the base of the Tree, she was among the first to set foot on the forest-floor of this new place. She stood for some time, a mild breeze ruffling her auburn hair, and thought. Or sommat like that, to Diggory's eye.

Diggory stood patiently nearby, and said not a word, nor made any movement that might interrupt.

'Mr. Stokey,' said the lady Ysabelon in time. 'In your experience, is this a familiar place?'

'I was never here before,' he answered. 'That I can be sure of.'

'I know that,' she said. 'I do not believe anybody has been here, for many years past. I meant to ask: is it familiar in its character? Does it remind you of any forest you ever set foot in before?'

A more complex question, that, requiring a touch more thought. Diggory didn't answer right away.

'I think not,' said he, having turned the matter over, in his slow way. 'On the face of it, I'd say yes, for while the lot of it is a mite bigger'n I'm used to, they're still trees. And it's still a forest. But...' His brow creased, as he groped for the words to express his next thought. 'It feels different. It don't feel like any forest I ever went into afore.'

Ysabelon nodded; the answer was as she had expected. 'A great deal lies hidden, I think.' This thought seemed to please, for she took a fresh look with a slight smile upon her pretty mouth, and took in a deep, contented breath.

'Aye,' said Diggory, following suit. 'Smells different, too.' There was the scent of earth and loam and fresh, green things, as one would expect of any forest. But sommat else was mixed up in there, too, though for *that* he surely had no words. It wasn't perfume, though it might be a little like a spring bouquet. It wasn't edible, though it vaguely reminded him of something he liked to eat. He breathed in deep again, and shrugged.

'There is much to discover,' said Ysabelon, her smile broadening. 'Come, Mr. Stokey. Perhaps you will lend me your company.'

She might have felt moved to say this because Diggory had stuck close, and made clear his intent to go on doing so. But her words brought out the bright smile in him, and he agreed with alacrity.

Then came Mother Gantry, clattering out of her house with a saucepan hanging from her belt, a thick cloak shrouding every other of her garments from view, the thickest and heaviest pair of boots Diggory had ever seen on a person, and (last but not least) the doughty expression of a woman ready for anything.

'Well, now,' said she, looking from Diggory to Ysabelon and back. 'What's the meaning of this? There's no call to be dancing sluggard-like on the doorstep, what with the Tree so pleased with itself. It's gone to a deal of trouble to get here, and us with it.'

'She,' murmured Diggory. 'That's a lady, Mother, if you please.'

Mother Gantry nodded once. 'That she must be, with her niceties and manners. Off we are, then.' She did not wait to see if Diggory or Ysabelon followed, but stamped away, her saucepan swinging with the rhythm of her stride, and clanking from time to time against some other, sturdy thing she imagined she'd have need of, and which Diggory couldn't see.

'A moment, Mother,' said Diggory, hastening to catch up. 'Shall we want this, do you think?' He tapped the pan, producing a hollow *thunk* of a sound.

'Who knows what we'll need, out there?' said Mother Gantry. 'I'll tell thee something, Diggory Stokey. Better to be over prepared than not at all.' She punctuated this statement with a meaningful, and disapproving, look at Diggory. 'We may chance to get hungry, and with no immediate way of returning to our Tree. And then what, if we've naught with us to cook in?'

Diggory judged it best not to pursue the point. Why, they'd nothing to put *in* the saucepan, nor anything to cook it *on*, come to that, but if it made Mother feel better to have a saucepan to hand, well, he could bear the clanking of the thing easily enough.

Ysabelon, he thought, was suppressing a smile, and doing a poor job of it.

He made her a sort of half-bow, a small gesture of

deference. 'Milady. Where shall we go, think you? Your eyes see farther than mine, I'll be bound.'

'I've had no Dream to guide me,' she said. 'Not of this part. But I think, perhaps…' She gazed a moment, then stepped away. 'Yonder direction,' said she, with a nod of her head.

Diggory, taking a long look, saw nothing there at all out of the way, or any different from everywhere else around. Enormous old trees rose far, far up into the clouds; a distant canopy of thick greenery shaded the ground; weeds and vines and fallen leaves covered the earth in places, though some parts were shadowed and bare.

He shrugged, though, and went along, for he had no better idea.

Mother Gantry, after a moment's stubborn trudging, altered the trajectory of her own steps, and fell in with theirs.

They made a quiet trio, for their eyes were too busy looking all around for their tongues to have much work to do. Diggory, his faith in Ysabelon's judgement knowing no bounds, expected every moment to happen upon something of note. Once or twice he heard an odd call, somewhere far off in the trees; a bird mayhap, though he never saw the creature that made the noise. For the most part, the forest was so silent as to be a mite unnerving, though he wouldn't have said so out loud. As though near everything in it were hiding, or slumbersome.

'Forgive me, lady,' said Diggory after a while, for a featureless trudge through undistinguished wilderness was not quite what he'd had in mind. 'But what led you to go this way?'

'I could not tell you,' she said slowly, and without

60

looking at him. 'I have not the words.'

'Oh.'

She paused, and glanced back the way they had come. Following the line of her gaze, Diggory could still make out the upper reaches of the Kottow Tree, falling away behind them.

'I wonder,' she murmured. 'If she knew—'

Diggory, still gazing upon the distant Tree, turned back just in time to witness a curious sight.

The lady Ysabelon vanished.

Not instantly. First, she *changed*, in no profound fashion, but Diggory would've sworn to it anyway. Perhaps she was a little taller, her hair a little brighter. Her red gown blew lightly about her legs, as though it were become lighter than air, and there being no wind at that moment to cause it.

He would have sworn, too, that there came a cold glitter in her hair and over the contours of her face, like droplets of frozen rain.

Then came the wind, a great billow of it, frigid as winter itself; and the lady walked through some unknowable thing, like a clear veil made of nothing at all, and disappeared.

'Milady?' said Diggory, standing rooted to the spot with horror.

Mother Gantry, engaged all the while in fiddling with the saucepan at her belt, looked up. 'We had ought to be sticking together,' said she. 'Where's the lady gone?'

'You cannot rightly think *I* should know,' answered Diggory, turning in a circle, but without catching so much as a glimpse of red cloth. 'When a lady vanishes into thin air—'

'Thin air?' Mother Gantry abandoned the problem

of the saucepan, and subjected the disobliging forest to a disapproving glare. 'Surely not, Diggory.'

'Surely so,' said he, thrusting out one arm to show her. 'How else do you explain this, Mother?'

Dusted over the brown cloth of his sleeve was a scattering of snowflakes, rapidly melting away.

Mother Gantry took in this improbable sight, her lips tightening. 'Ill-mannered, I call that.' She raised her voice, and before Diggory could object to the *lady's* being termed anything such, she clarified this statement by shouting, as loudly as she could, 'Give her back, now! We've need of her.'

'Who are you talking to?' whispered Diggory.

'Whatever rude, magic thing as has stolen her away,' answered Mother Gantry, frowning. 'Someone has done it, and they shall *un*do it, if I've anything to say about it.'

But nobody answered her. Certainly nothing and no one stepped forward to own up to the offence, and produce the lady, bemused perhaps but unharmed.

Diggory heard only a faint whisper of wind, a thin gust, like an airy sigh.

'Right.' Diggory stood in what passed, with him, for profound thought. No feeble-witted man, he, but not quick of thought either; he'd capacity enough for deep reflection, if given a moment or two.

Mother Gantry, having had the knowing of him some few years now, let him have his thinkings in silence.

'Right,' said Diggory again, and nodded. 'We'll be needin' Maut.'

'Maut? Why she?'

'Because there is something mighty *fey* about all

this, or my name ain't Diggory Stokey. Maut Fey is the woman we need.'

'I'd have a mind to go for the Wizard, myself,' said Mother Gantry.

'The Wizard, whoever he may be, has shown no interest in comin' down,' said Diggory. 'I've a suspicion he ain't up there. Maut it is.'

With which words, he turned about, until his eye fell once again on the reaching boughs of the Kottow Tree, and thither he went.

He and Mother Gantry, moving at a smartish pace, covered this distance in no time, and arrived to find Maut Sweetlove surrounded by squirrels in coats of red, black and white. She'd just fed them, by the looks, for a fine feast was in full swing. Maut herself stood nearby, checking her pockets for sommat. Gower Bordekin was with her.

'Maut!' called Diggory, breaking into a laborious trot. 'You must come at once. We've grave need of you.'

'Why, are you got into trouble already?' said Maut, though her humorous smile faded when she saw the real concern in Diggory's face. 'What's amiss?'

'The lady,' said Diggory, stopping before her, and catching his breath. 'Gone.'

'You mean she has gone off alone? Diggory, I understand your feelings but she is well able to manage for herself.'

Diggory stood shaking his head all through this speech. 'Not like that. *Gone*. Walked through a gust of wind and disappeared.'

'What?'

He thrust out his arm to show her the snow, all that Ysabelon's passage had left behind, but of course it was long melted. 'I had snow here,' he said. 'And *she* was all over ice, or some such, twinklin' like stars, and then she was gone.'

Gower Bordekin, having listened thus far in silence, looked up at that. 'Ice?'

Diggory nodded again. 'I think so. I didn't get more'n a glimpse afore she was gone.'

'Show me,' said Gower.

Away went the whole party, a quartet now, Mother Gantry and Diggory and Gower and Maut Fey. Diggory led them back through the Trees, until they came upon the unremarkable spot where Ysabelon had vanished. Still there was nothing to set it apart from the rest of the forest, not that Diggory could see. A little clearing it was, between three great trees, with a quantity of leaves all about, and a vine or two clambering up the trunks.

'I see no ice,' said Gower, walking about, and examining the ground with his keen eyes.

'The lady took it with her,' said Diggory.

'Are you certain?' said Gower Bordekin. The question, though, did not strike Diggory as asked in doubt, or scepticism. He had an urgent way about him, as though the matter were important for some reason beyond the fate of the lady Ysabelon.

'Aye,' said Diggory firmly. 'I'd not imagine that.'

'Not a boy of much imagination at all, our Diggory,' said Mother Gantry, patting Diggory on the back as she spoke.

Gower paced back and forth, laying his hands against the boles of the trees, and scuffing the earth with his feet. 'Nothing's here to see now,' he said, and disappeared.

Diggory missed it, that time. It was Maut who

gasped, and when Diggory looked up, there was Gower Bordekin all gone and vanished.

'Well, and ain't that grand,' said Diggory. 'But you'll have seen it, now? The ice, and the snow?'

Maut said, 'I — I saw —'

'What, Maut?' said Diggory.

'It wasn't ice,' said she, staring at nothing, as though her eyes might, with enough will, cut through the semblance of the forest about her, and see into wherever it was Ysabelon and Gower had gone. 'It was a light, all golden, like high noon. And a wind, yes, but *warm*.'

'That can't be right,' said Diggory, knowing it for a fatuous remark as he spoke, for what was *right* about anything in this Tree-drowned place? 'Not a single snowflake? What then did *you* see?'

'I saw — Summer,' said she simply, and looked at Diggory with spellbound eyes. 'He has gone in to Summer.'

CHAPTER TWO

Maut did not know, when she looked at Diggory, that her own eyes shone with a glow of reflected summer; that motes of a dulcet fire burned there, just for an instant, before she turned away.

Nor could she have said why, when *she* had witnessed the vanishment of Gower Bordekin, she had seen so much more than had Diggory. Whether it was because the folk of the Kottow Tree were right, when they called her Maut Fey (an unwelcome idea), or whether happenstance alone had made it so, she did not choose to guess.

But when a soft summer breeze wound Gower Bordekin in its gentle embrace and swept him away, Maut saw exactly whither he had gone.

He'd changed, too. Most would call Gower a well-looking man, she thought, with his tall stature and his muscled might. But with Summer all around him, striding off into the heart of magic with one boot yet in Maut's world, she'd seen another Gower. One whose manly frame had transcended that of a mere mortal, so much latent power had she seen in him at that moment. There had been nothing like ice-rain or unseasonable snow to mark him out as altered; nothing so clear as that. But Summer had taken him for her own, and soft Summer magic shone from every part of the man.

He was just as obviously unaware of it himself.

Maut had seen another forest beyond him, like the one in which she stood, yet also unlike. The trees of this other forest were similar to those around her, at least in height and girth, but their bark bore the colours of her spice-jars at home: ginger and cinnamon, and clove. A rain of *something* had drifted gently down, but she did not think it was water. Petals, belike, the colours of honey and cream; or perhaps the smallest of leaves, torn from who-knew-what, and sent wafting about upon the breeze. A strong light, all green-and-gold, had lit everything with a glow to warm the heart as much as the body.

She had felt the heat, even from some few feet away. And there came the only *wrong* note, in this balmy vision: there had been too much heat, too fierce, too brutal. Such a burning warmth rightly belonged to a desert.

Gower had seemed untouched by it. He'd gone striding off without pause, as though naught were amiss, or as though he saw nothing so.

And then something had closed up behind him, hiding him even from Maut's sight, and he was gone.

She tried to alter this, as she described, in halting words, her Seeings to Diggory. The pair of them made right fools of themselves (in Mother Gantry's view), walking back and forth and around in circles like a couple of chickens, trying without success to make whatever had happened for Ysabelon and Gower happen also for them. Perhaps the hapless pair had stepped on something, or passed something by, that had opened the way to wherever they'd gone. If Maut or Diggory could retrace those steps, mayhap they could fetch them out again.

But nothing so simple could be the cause, for Maut herself walked the precise way Gower had gone, placing her feet in the footprints he had left, and naught occurred.

'Well,' she said at last, having repeated this process some few times through, without result. 'Like it or not, it's not *us* as is wanted in there.'

'In where, though?' said Diggory. 'By your account, it's the same forest they're in, only a bit different.'

Maut smothered a laugh. 'A bit! *One* being hotter than any high summer I've known, and in the other it's raining ice, and you call it a *bit* different?'

'Aye,' said Diggory stubbornly. 'For the rest is much the same. 'Tis only the weather that's odd.'

It wasn't just the weather, but Maut could scarcely explain that to herself, let alone to Diggory. She let the matter lie. 'What think you, Mother?' said she instead. 'You're the headwoman of the Tree. Should we go after these two? Or consider as they deserves whatever they get, for leaving us behind?'

'Surely thou hast no *will* to go in there?' said Mother Gantry, shocked. 'It sounds right strange, and not at all nice, what with the heat. Or the cold.'

'Then Gower might like us to fetch him back, no?' said Maut.

'And the lady,' put in Diggory. 'She's in no wise dressed for that kind of inclement weather.'

'Seems to me as that's the wrong question,' said Mother Gantry. 'Whatever they may be thinking, we've got no notion of it, and no way to reach them either. Well, then. What *can* we do?'

That stymied Maut, she having just spent quarter of an hour demonstrating only what they could *not*.

Diggory was looking at her. Full of hope.

'What is it, Diggory?' she sighed.

'We must rely on you, Maut Fey,' said he. 'If anyone's got eyes to see, it's you.'

'That's nice,' said she, sourly, 'and quite foolish, for if I could see aught of use just now I'd have told you, would I not?'

The man appeared crestfallen, which irritated, for she felt responsible for dashing his hopes even if she'd not done so by her own choice.

'Come, we know of others somewhere up the Tree, with a fairer claim to fey blood than I,' she offered. 'Don't we? What of Mudleaf, and Willow Wildboots, if it's fey you want? What of them?'

Diggory brightened.

'Not that I know where you're going with that manner of thought,' she cautioned. 'Just because they are fey in no wise means they know aught about what's afoot here.'

'True,' said Diggory. 'But it's something we can do.'

'Something we can *try*,' amended Maut.

'Good,' said Mother Gantry. 'That's thinking like sensible people.'

But Maut, having turned to retrace her steps, stopped again. 'I'd like to mark this spot,' she said. 'None of us can see anything strange about it, but nonetheless, we've had two people vanish in the same place.'

'But gone on to different destinations,' pointed out Mother Gantry.

'I can't explain it either,' said Maut, stripping a ribbon from her hair, and tying it around a low-hanging bough near where Gower had disappeared. 'But I'd not like to lose this one clue, such as it is.'

This done, she went on again. 'To find Mudleaf, then,' she said. 'Which might be somewhat difficult. Last I saw of *them*, they'd wandered off.'

They were not to find Mudleaf or Willow Wildboots. Not then. For the two fey had more than the eyes to see the reality behind the veil (or the glamour behind the truth). They had the boots to walk those roads, and the unerring steps to take them straight into the heart of magic in that lost, old forest.

Not that either of them knew it themselves.

'This is looking a mite odd,' said Mudleaf, when she and Willow had been all a-wander among the riotous Trees for some time, without finding themselves anywhere of use.

'*Now* you think it odd?' scoffed Willow, still carting some leafery about with him: a striped one the size of his face, and several more in curlicue shapes, all frosted around the edges.

'Right enough,' agreed Mudleaf. 'More odd, is what I meant. Look here.' She planted her feet, and pointed one long, knobbly finger at the earth between her boots.

Willow came over, tucking his leafery under one arm, and looked down.

'See that?' said Mudleaf.

'A snail?' said Willow.

'No.'

Willow poked something with the toe of one shoe. 'Either you're seeing things,' he decided, 'or I am. I can't decide which. But there's nothing here but a snail.'

'It is no snail but a flower,' insisted Mudleaf. 'Growing all over the ground, only unless I miss my guess it's made of frost.' She tilted her head, gazed a moment, and amended, 'Maybe snow.' A fine carpet it made, too, spread out like an embroidered rug, pale grey of leaf and all over rime. Tiny white blooms — *snow* white, thought Mudleaf, only in truth, not merely in hue — were dotted hither and thereabout, trembling in the breeze. 'I don't know how it doesn't melt,' she added. 'Especially given what's happening over there.' She used the ladle this time, and a fine pointing-tool it made, permitting her to indicate an adjacent patch not far from Willow's feet. 'See you *that?*'

Willow turned about. 'No,' he said shortly. 'Just a lot of green-like.'

'Then it's my turn for madness,' said Mudleaf. 'Or maybe for reason, who can know? There's nothing green there at all, Willow. It is all over dandelions, but they're made of gold, and they shine.'

Willow narrowed his eyes. 'Green, still,' he reported, with a sigh. 'It's your turn for the wild eyes indeed, but I wish you'd give them back. If one of them birds comes by, I might miss it now.'

'There's one,' said Mudleaf, pointing her ladle towards the sky. An ethereal birdling sailed over their heads, its plumage azure and riverwater-blue. Only, when it passed over the spot where the ice-blossoms grew, it went all over frost, its feathers turning snowy and downy. Then, it caught the sunshine in the dandelion-patch, spraying out light like droplets of topaz. It hurt to look upon those butter-yellow feathers; Mudleaf shaded her eyes.

When she looked again, the bird had got its river-colours back, and away it went.

'Willow,' said she. 'I am minded to try a thing.'

'A thing?' said he, and looked upon her, all suspicion. 'Without me?'

'No, you've to help me. Watch.' Before she could think better of so bold (or foolish) a step, she set one booted foot deeper into the frost-blossom patch, and walked through, one slow step at a time. And she grew colder in the doing of it; it seemed to her that a gale howled past her ears, singing of cold and frozen things, and the frost caught at her boots and clambered up her legs.

But no sooner had she set her feet among the dandelions than it all melted away. The wind turned warm — no, *hot*, and blistering. The light both gladdened and blinded her eyes; she sweated her way through several more strides, her nose full of the scent of pollen and her ears lulled by the sounds of droning bees.

Then she was through. The light tilted and sank; green verdure returned.

Mudleaf looked back, and saw — nothing but cool, shaded green.

'Interesting,' said she. 'What are your dull eyes seeing now, Willow?'

'Dull?' spluttered he. 'Was it not *me* that saw all the magic before now?'

'Aye, but then I stole it away, and I'll not give it back.' Mudleaf grinned.

'How did you do so? I'll steal it back!' Willow raised a small fist.

'I jest, I jest,' said Mudleaf, brandishing her ladle. 'If I took the glamour from your eyes, it wasn't by my own design. But answer my question, now. What do you see on *me*?'

'Nothing untoward,' said he, sullenly.

'Glamour, then,' said Mudleaf. 'Not a thing of it was real.' But then she glanced down, and beheld the state of her skirt. Clinging to the cobweb strands were a lot of dandelion-spew: fat brown seeds with their lacy parasols aloft, hitching a lift with the fey-thing. The clocks had dispersed themselves all over her.

'Look at that, now!' she crowed, picking a few off, and flicking them at Willow. 'You see *that*, don't you?'

Willow captured one, and frowned at it. 'Where'd you get that? I've not seen a dandelion since last spring.'

'Here,' said Mudleaf, indicating the heat-shimmery spot with a wave of her ladle. Or where it had been until a moment ago, anyway. 'Lots of the blighters there, or they were up 'till a moment gone. Think. Here's a thought.' She tramped her way around the bole of a large tree until she stood in much the place she'd begun from. Then she repeated her walk again.

There was the rime-carpet come back, and the dandelions too.

'Hither, Willow!' she called. 'Walk where I walk, and put your feet where there's been mine.' The little fellow followed in her wake, and she knew from the sounds he made that he saw it all *now*.

'It's not that about bespelling the eyes,' said she. 'All a matter of perspective. Stand but two inches off the Right Spot, and it's all gone.'

'But why?' said Willow, swatting at a dandelion clock. The seeds puffed loose and streamed away, whisked off by a playful wind.

'A right good question,' said Mudleaf. 'I don't know. But I think me we'll go on this way.' Arm stretched out, ladle marking the route, Mudleaf strode on as she'd started: straight and true.

This time, the dandelions did not fade, and the drab green of it all did not return. Every time a hint of green ventured in, Mudleaf adjusted her steps, until it went off again. By this means, she found a road that went on and on in the sun-drenched heat — until the cold came back, and the ice, and swept it away into winter.

'Well,' said she after a while, when she and Willow had paused to melt the ice off their clothes, and trade their shivers for a sun-baking. 'What think you best, Willow? The heat or the cold?'

Willow dithered. 'A bit of both, by preference,' he decided. 'Mixed together-like, to something bearable.'

'Can't do that,' said Mudleaf shortly. 'Choose just the one.'

'Cold, then,' sighed Willow. 'The sunlight hurts my eyes.'

'Right.' Mudleaf looked and looked, until she found a space where the rime glittered diamond-bright, and the snow fell swift and thick. 'This way,' she said. 'And look, there's one of your birdlings leading the way.'

The bird drifted far overhead. It could not be that the *birdling* made the snow, of course; that wasn't the way things worked at all. But it looked mighty like it. Wings the length of Mudleaf spread all the way out, beating a gentle rhythm upon the wind; and with every airy movement, down came another flurry of snow.

'Following the snowling, then,' said Mudleaf, pausing only to deliver a swift kick to Willow's ankles, for the fool boy had paused to watch the bird's slow progress and stood there with his jaw hanging open. 'Sharpish, or you'll freeze where you stand. On!'

Willow yelped, followed this with an unflattering observation on Mudleaf's probable parentage — a thought that only made Mudleaf cackle — and hastened on. The two of them pelted off in the snowling's wake, at no lackadaisical pace; for though the bird flew slowly, the thing was far larger than they, and with their small legs they had no easy time keeping up.

'It's mighty c-cold,' stuttered Willow, after no more than a few minutes.

'That comes as a surprise, does it?'

'N-no, though I do believe as it's getting w-worse.'

Mudleaf, unable to contest this point, said nothing. It *was* growing worse, rapidly so. She'd not had cause before to consider her own attire insufficient, for she had layers and layers of silks and leafery and cobweb, and they had always served her well before.

Not now. The cold deepened with every second step, and Mudleaf felt the rime coating her clothes and her face, thickening with every gust of the snowling's wings.

'Mayhap we should turn back,' said she, searching for a glimpse of the sun-baked dandelion field, or even the cool green shade of the forest. Neither blessed her.

Not that there weren't beauties enough, to distract a person from an imminent freezing. Once fairly upon the snowling's path, the quantities of frost-blooms grew apace, clambering heedless over all Mudleaf saw. And she saw spires of snow and ice, glittering in the distance; nearer to her, a wide road of beaten silver, impervious, somehow, to the snow; and either side of it rose the ice-gilded walls of a city.

No, not a city. Mudleaf realised that, snowfall notwithstanding, they were not outside. They had come into a grand hall, roofed far above their heads with something clear, like glass — or maybe not roofed at all. Their snowling had fellows far up there, spiralling aloft, and leaving ice-flurries in their wake.

Nearer eye-level, she saw low divans clad in ice-white velvet. Silver-wrought tables groaned under the weight of more crystal dishes than Mudleaf could hope to count, overflowing with rime-dusted fruits. Long windows looked out over a kingdom of snow-drowned houses, little to be seen of them but an outline of eaves here, the glint of a window there. They had a silenced look about them; no one stirred out there, no footprints marred the purity of the fallen snow.

Such people as there were congregated in the grand hall. Some of them lounged indolently upon those divans, listlessly sorting through dishes of fragrant sweets: Mudleaf could smell them from where she stood, all redolent of plum-wine and rosewater as they were. Others paced, their velvet slippers and the hems of their silken gowns stirring up snow with every step. They were not like Mudleaf. Taller by far, they were white as snow themselves, with a cruel glitter to their cool, distant eyes.

They looked up, as Mudleaf and Willow approached.

'And now we've a visitor,' said one voice, a lady, in no pleased fashion. 'Two of them, no less. What, are we to be invaded by outlanders at last?'

'Peace, Peronel,' said another, a mile-high gent who got in Mudleaf's way, and stared down at her like a glacier himself. 'They will not last long. I marvel that they yet move at all.'

Mudleaf came to a stop, and got hold of Willow's arm to stop him too. 'W-we came from the f-forest,' she said through frozen lips. 'And we'd like to g-go back, if you please.'

'The forest?' Peronel swept into view, a leggy creature all draped in velvets of a fine blue. 'The *forest*? That cannot be.'

'W-what?' said Mudleaf, her teeth chattering. 'Why not?'

Peronel exchanged a look with her friend. 'Where do you claim this "forest" lies?'

Mudleaf turned about, and swept out an arm. 'Back there,' she said, 'where we came from.' But the words made no sense, for behind her now there was only more of the grand hall; it went on and on, as near forever as Mudleaf could tell. Even in the farthest depths that her eyes could see, cold white lights twinkled.

'Perhaps,' said the other one, 'the snow speaks truly. Perhaps *she* is returned.'

'No,' snapped Peronel. 'If that were true, where is she?'

Mudleaf, finding this conversation impossible to follow, grew distracted. Willow had elbowed her in the ribs; once her attention was gained, he pointed mutely at a thing over to the left, a piece of hugeness Mudleaf had taken for a pillar, or some such.

'It's a Tree,' hissed Willow.

Mudleaf wanted to squash so foolish an idea at once, but a nearer glance told her he was right. Piled around the base of the towering thing, hiding what roots there may be, was a deep bank of snow. Rising from it, the trunk; not so thick in girth as that of their own, dear Tree, but not so far off, either. A ways up there, over Mudleaf's head, she saw a door set into the bark, though so coated in ice was it that she doubted it would open.

'What have you d-done to that Tree?' she said, interrupting Peronel's argument with her friend.

'Done?' said Peronel, after a moment's silence. '*We* have done nothing to it.'

'How c-comes it to be there, right in the middle of this hall?' pursued Mudleaf. 'And why's it f-f-frozen solid?'

'All things freeze, in Lady Frost's kingdom.' 'Twas Peronel's friend who spoke those words, and with a cruel curl to his lips that Mudleaf did not like.

'*You* haven't,' she managed, though her face was so cold she almost couldn't move her lips at all.

'But you have,' said he, softly. 'Little Summertide things ought not to come into the Winter.'

Mudleaf shook so hard with the cold that her teeth rattled in her head. 'I'll n-not f-f-freeze,' she insisted. 'And I'll not stay another minute where I'm n-not w-w-wanted. Come, W-willow.' She turned smartish-like, and strode off back the way she'd come, to the forest, and the Kottow Tree. If her feet had found the way into this dismal place, they could find the way out again.

But Willow didn't follow. He did not move at all, and a glance told Mudleaf the reason: he was all over hoarfrost, like a leaf in winter, and frozen solid beneath.

'W-w-we w-will—' she began, but Lady Frost's minions got her, too. Rime crawled up her legs and her torso, and grew over her face; she went cold as an icicle within.

Her last thought, before the snow dulled her senses entirely, was one of regret. If only they had taken the dandelion-road, instead. She might have fried alive like a cracked egg in the desert, but at least she'd not have made a statue for the amusement of *these* high-and-mighty folk.

CHAPTER THREE

'I don't mean to complain,' said Diggory, 'but a man could grow tired of walkin' in circles, you know.'

'Keeping thy mouth closed would be more to the purpose, Diggory,' answered Mother Gantry, tart as a crab-apple.

'Aren't you tired yet, Mother?' said he. 'Maut, let us cease this traipsin' about. It's of no use, and Mother's weary.'

Mother Gantry fixed him with a glare, but she did not contradict him.

Maut saw and heard all this with an inward sigh, and capitulated. Diggory spoke truly. Mother Gantry may be a game old lady, but old lady she was; and they *had* been walking in circles. That she had led them on such a route in hopes of happening upon Mudleaf and Willow Wildboots wasn't much to the purpose, if they found nobody.

'Well, you're right,' she conceded, stopping beside a grand beech tree, and gazing up into the far-off canopy. 'But what would you suggest instead, hm?

We'll get nothing done by standing here, either.'

'Mudleaf ain't to be found,' said Diggory. 'So we must have another plan.'

'To achieve what?' said Mother Gantry.

'To get the lady Ysabelon back,' said Diggory.

'And Gower,' put in Maut.

Mother Gantry gave a sigh, and lowered her aching bones to the ground. A small hillock, covered over with vinery, afforded her some semblance of a perch, and she rested her back against the beech's broad trunk. 'Mayhap they've no wish to be brought back,' she offered. 'Hast thou thought of that?'

Maut and Diggory looked long at one another. They hadn't.

'But how shall we know, if we don't find them?' Diggory asked.

'For my part, I'm for going home,' said Mother, without answering this.

'You mean... back to Kottow?' said Diggory, appalled.

'I liked Kottow. There was a place that made *sense*. But no, Diggory Stokey, I don't mean Kottow. I speak of our Tree. *There's* home.'

Maut thought this over. 'You know, you've maybe an idea there. After all, if anybody could walk us straight into wherever Gower's gone—'

'And the lady,' put in Diggory.

'—then it'd have to be the Tree as walked us into this forest, surely.'

'Ah,' said Diggory, raising a finger. 'Do you happen to remember where we left it, at that?'

'It's that way,' said Mother Gantry, pointing.

'How'd you know that, Mother?' said Diggory, having looked, and (like Maut) seen nothing in that direction to point the way.

'Because *thou* mayst have more hair than wit, but I've more wit than hair.' The old lady levered herself to her feet again, assisted by Maut. 'Make haste, for the air's changed. I believe we are to have rain.'

She was soon proved right. With Mother Gantry in the lead, the group's pace was of necessity slow, and they had not gone so very far before a few fat, cold droplets of rain came sailing down through any break in the canopy that offered. One fell on Maut's cheek.

Without breaking stride, Mother unlaced the saucepan from its loop upon her belt, and held it up over her head. The next few raindrops that came down bounced off its broad base, and left her dry.

'The pan's of use after all,' remarked Diggory, with a wink to Maut.

'As I told thee,' said Mother Gantry calmly.

Neither Maut nor Diggory having equipped themselves with a saucepan, the best they could do was pull up the hoods of their cloaks, and trust to wax-coatings and the thick canopy above to keep them from getting wet through.

The rain was no light, spring shower, though. Within five minutes, the noise it made drumming against the thick leafery above was such as to reach their ears, even so far below; a distant clamour promising a thorough wetting to come.

'Eaugh!' said Mother Gantry a moment later, having taken an unwary step into a brightish patch with no canopy over it. Here, the rain came gushing down, striking the emerald verdure below with force enough to send up lancing sparks of bright water. Mother had got a faceful of it, Maut judged, the saucepan having no brim to speak of.

The old lady, undaunted, adjusted her steps, and made to go around; but Maut stopped her with a light grip upon her elbow. 'Wait.'

'What is it now?' said Mother.

'It's raining,' said Maut.

'I noticed that.'

'No, look,' said Diggory, and gently turned Mother about to face the rain-dewed clearing again.

What had been an abundance of emerald-hued vegetation had grown bored of its monochrome clothes, belike, and fancied a change. All sapphire about, it now was, with veins of amethyst; then a brilliant topaz, with traces of ruby, and so on, through many a wash of colour. The effect was spreading, too, florid flashes of gaudy giddiness passing from leaf to leaf, taking in ground first at a creeping pace, and then in great leaps. Soon, the earth under Maut's feet was all over madness, and so was she.

'That tree,' said Diggory in awe.

Maut followed his gaze. It wasn't the same beech under which they had so recently sheltered, but it could have been its twin — at least, at first. But once the rain had got all the way down the trunk, it ceased to be only a beech. Maut saw oak and ash and birch leaves drifting down with the rain, many of them odd-coloured.

Then came a rumbling in the earth, some disturbance deep below that Maut couldn't see. But she saw it when the beech-tree (as was) began a-shaking, like the Kottow Tree at home; she saw the thing swell in girth and doubtless height, in the space of a few breaths; she saw the huge, knotted roots ripple like water, and shift, and then the tree tore itself loose in a spray of damp earth.

Off it went.

'I'm almost certain that was only a tree, 'till a moment ago,' whispered Diggory.

'It was,' said Maut. She pointed out another, a bit farther off. 'So was that.'

All around them, grand old trees were shaking off inertia, and setting off for a turn about the forest. The ground shuddered and cracked under the force of so much movement, and the tumult of so many booming steps hurt Maut's ears.

'We'll be squashed,' said she, whisking Mother Gantry out of the way of a flying root. 'Quick, we must get back to our own Tree!'

There followed a stumbling, shambling flight through the wandering forest, dodging roots, brushing off a rain of leaves almost as heavy as that of the water.

'I've lost my bearings!' wailed Mother after a while. 'Everything's changed!'

Diggory tripped over a flailing root and went face-down into the earth. Maut hauled him up again. 'I'd suggest we take shelter!' she called. 'But I wouldn't know where.'

No shelter offered. It seemed as though half the trees in the forest had pulled up their roots and gone a-walking. Butterflies the size of Maut's head settled on branches here-and-there, and clustered up and down trunks, all of them sun-coloured or ice-coloured or whatnot else; one alighted upon Maut's hair, and refused to be shaken off for some time. One took a fancy to Mother Gantry's saucepan, still clutched tightly in one of her fists, and rode inside it for a space.

There were birds, too, great leggy things with a

wingspan as wide as Maut was tall. The things swooped about as heedless as the trees, sprinkling more of the rain all everywhere with their wing-beats.

'We're doomed,' moaned Diggory, though to his credit, for all his despair he kept Mother Gantry shielded as best he could. 'We're to be pounded to juice under a horde of barmy trees.'

'No!' shouted Maut, catching a glimpse of a heartening sight. 'There's our Tree!'

It wasn't to be expected that the Kottow Tree would hold itself still and quiet, when all its comrades were gadding about. It was on the hoof, same as the rest; but Maut could swear it was coming for them all of a-purpose, for when she shouted, the Tree changed its course — waltzing gracefully out of the way of a rampaging oak — and pounded over their way. Mercifully, it had all its doors held tightly shut, so that nothing fell out.

The Tree slowed as it neared the hapless trio, and stopped. Its branches stuck out, wide and bristling, as though to repel the advances of its arboreal neighbours.

Mother Gantry's door creaked open a crack.

'Quick, Mother,' said Diggory. 'In we go.' They got Mother safely in first; Maut shoved Diggory into the trunk after her.

Up she went at last, collecting three startled squirrels on her way, and all but fell into Mother Gantry's kitchen.

The door closed upon them, and some of the deafening tumult faded.

'Maut,' said Diggory, after he'd caught his breath. 'There's something you should know.'

'What's that?' said Maut absently, her attention all

for a white little squirrel, shivering with fright, and tucking itself into her tunic.

Diggory held out his own hands and slowly turned them over, then extended this scrutiny to his legs and arms and torso. 'I think I'm all right,' he said. 'But you, Maut. Something's happened to *you*.'

'This is no time to be mysterious,' Maut snapped. '*What* has happened to me?'

'Your — your ears,' Diggory faltered. 'And your hair, and your eyes —'

Instinctively, Maut clutched at the first two of these articles, without it much enlightening her. 'What about them?'

'They're all odd-coloured,' said Diggory. 'Your hair, that is, and your eyes. It's as though you've been... drinking the sunlight, or some such.' He flushed, embarrassed at so flowery a phrase having popped out of his ordinary mouth.

'Diggory—' said Maut, in exasperation.

'And thine ears,' put in Mother Gantry. 'Which always were a bit odd, forgive me for saying so. Now they're more so.'

'*More* odd?' Maut felt up the curve of her left ear, and paused. What had been a slight curl at the tip was much more pronounced. 'But,' she said numbly. 'But I didn't feel a thing. When it... happened.'

'Mightn't be real,' Diggory offered. 'Just a glamour, like. They say as the fair folk can do that.'

'We haven't seen any fair folk,' Mother Gantry disagreed. 'Well — unless you count Maut, here.'

'But I'm not,' said Maut, distantly, as though she experienced the conversation from a remove of several feet. 'I'm still me.'

'You don't look it,' said Diggory. 'And why has the

rain got into *your* skin, when it hasn't done a thing to Mother and me?'

Maut had no answer for this, of course. She stared at Diggory and Mother Gantry, bereft of words; feeling only a sinking conviction within, that nothing was ever going to be quite the same again.

And if Diggory had had leisure to notice, he might have observed that not *quite* all was well with Mother, either. Her face might not have changed, much; but a look of befuddlement had crept into the space behind her eyes, as though all the certainties of yester eve had been all washed away.

PART THREE
THE WINTER COURT

CHAPTER ONE

The vanished lady did not know herself to be so; not at first.

If the ice-rain settled like mist over her face and hair, and kissed the pale skin there, she did not feel it. Nor the winter's wind that swirled around her legs, making sport with her skirt. What had so impressed themselves upon Diggory's eyes passed Ysabelon's senses by.

She crossed the unknowable divide (in Diggory's vague ideas) in the space of one step to the next, unconscious of any great change. Some few more steps she travelled before a realisation dawned, and then, of course, it was too late.

'I wonder if she knew—' she'd been saying to Diggory, when it had happened. 'I wonder if she—' (meaning the Kottow Tree) '—knew something that we did not,' was the sentence. 'Something about *us*, and this place—'

Then it struck her that all had gone awry. Not because of the freezing wind that howled around this ice-bound place (for she felt it not), but because after the third step she'd taken, the fourth landed her in snow up to her ankles. She felt *that*, an unsteadying sinking sensation, where her foot had expected to encounter solid ground.

Then the daydreams cleared from her befogged eyes, and she saw where she was come to: a forest still, inevitably, but one snow-drowned and all a-glitter with crystalline ice. The vast boles of ancient trees were securely planted amid the snow; no wandering about for *these* hoary old souls. They bore the hushed, deep-winter air of trees that had not felt the touch of spring in a hundred years. Flurries of snow danced in spiralling gusts from one trunk to another; a gentle rain of frost came dulcetly down.

To Ysabelon's ears, the wind *sang*.

She paused a while, taking in this silent scene, and the surprise she felt upon beholding it was not so profound after all. She'd seen snow, in her mystifying, magic-touched Dreams. Snow, and frost, and endless ice, and just such a winter-clad forest as this.

The lady Ysabelon turned, once, and found herself alone: neither Diggory Stokey nor Mother Gantry's steps had brought them into this place.

Well, then.

She went on, step by step into the blanketing snow, and every sound she made was muffled in the stillness. Even the soft *crunch* of the snow compacting under her footfalls scarcely penetrated the silence. All that she heard was that wind, singing snow-songs to itself as it swept the frost from the low-hanging boughs, and sent it whirling into the sky.

A frost-flurry danced Ysabelon's way, and stayed, kept pace with her as she trudged determinedly on.

Another joined them, and a third, until a leaping entourage centred around the lady, attending her every step.

'Hello,' she said, after a time, for in their playfulness they seemed to be more than mere eddies of air hung with velvet ice. 'Can you tell me where I am come to?'

No one answered her. Ysabelon went on, untroubled. Just as she had known her fate to lie with the Kottow Tree, she felt at home in this forest; a sense of inevitability, as though the strangeness, for her, had lain in her former life in the towns of Lambelin and Oakham, and Ryle. *Here* was everything made right again, or soon to be, though she could not have said how.

There was a peace in that, despite her solitary state.

It did not occur to her to find it strange, either, when her struggles lessened, her movement eased. Her feet ceased to sink into the depths of the snow, for gusts of wind caught about her ankles, gifting her steps with a buoyancy that lifted her above such toil. This, too, seemed natural; she wondered only that it had not always been so, with her.

On she went in this fashion for some time, while the frost-flurries caught up her cloak and sent it billowing out behind her, and the snow spun ice-jewels in her hair.

At length, the blanketing hush lessened, for distant sounds reached her ears. Voices drifting upon the wind, shouts and merriment. Music, besides that made by the wind itself.

Ysabelon came to the bank of a great river, unfolding between the trees like a wide road paved in ice, for the rushing waters were frozen solid. A fair was in progress upon that wintry expanse: a great jumble of stalls set every which way, without reason or design, as though dropped wherever their vendors happened to stand. Awnings of cobweb and moth-silk hung over each one, decked in icy dew, and the wares they offered were of a similar character: brooches of ice-white leaves rimed in frost; cobweb cloaks; clear goblets of something fragrant that steamed in the chill air, pouring out streams of white mist.

The Frost Fair. The words came to Ysabelon's mind, without source, save perhaps some long-ago Dream.

One wizened old tree stood right at the water's edge, its branches spanning almost the entire width of the river. Lights hung there, cold-white and bright, and more leaves than a tree had business keeping hold of, in the winter. These were silver-etched and pale, and odd: irregular of shape, as though the tree had not grown them herself, but had been gifted with them by some warm-hearted soul, who pitied the tree's naked state.

This tree was not empty. A great many people were gathered there, seated upon its gnarled branches and singing songs to the stars. Some were like Ysabelon herself: tall and long of limb, though not all were pale as she. Others were but half of her height, if not less, and as wrinkled and sere as the tree.

Many other such folk milled about the river, buying goods from the Fair (or selling them). Some turned to look at Ysabelon as she drew near, and a murmur went up.

Ysabelon bore this scrutiny with untouched serenity, for there was no menace in it. 'I am come to the Frost Fair, I think?' she said, once fairly in the midst of the frozen water.

'Aye,' said a rough-looking woman barely three feet high, clad in a gown of earth-coloured stuff, and wearing (incongruously) a wreath of snowflakes in her hair. 'Yer just in time.' This thought was productive of mirth, for some reason, for she went off into a peal of it, a nasty, grating sound.

But her neighbour observed Ysabelon much more closely, with narrowed eyes, and awarded her companion a swift elbow to the ribs. 'Watch yer tongue,' said this second woman, shorter and stouter than the first, and wreathed in flaxen shawls of myriad hue. 'Don't ye know who yer talking to?'

The cackler stopped cackling, but gave an insolent shrug, sublimely uninterested. 'Can't see as it matters.'

'The wind,' said the second woman. 'And the snow, and the frost. Best be polite to *them*, or you won't see the spring.'

'Spring?' said the cackler, and went off cackling again. 'Chance'd be a fine thing.'

'Has there been no spring?' asked Ysabelon.

The second woman, with her shawls all about her, smiled upon Ysabelon in a kindly way. 'Well, but what would we want with spring, anyhow?' said she. 'Couldn't have our Frost Fair, then, could we?'

The two drifted away, pausing only at a nearby vendor to purchase pale wine in a frosted bottle (for one) and a second wreath of snowflakes (for the other). But they did not give money for these treasures; Ysabelon saw a grubby twig handed over, and a handful of dead leaves. These worthless trifles the vendor accepted with a grin and an obsequious bow.

'What about you, lady?' said the wine-seller, his eye

alighting upon Ysabelon. 'I see you've no need of pretties for yer hair, but how about a sip of ice-wine? Chill you nicely, our wine.' He winked.

'I believe I am chilled enough already,' said Ysabelon, politely, and wondered why a titter went up, among those assembled around her.

'I reckon you are, at that,' said the wine-seller, and made her a bow every bit as obsequious as that he had bestowed upon the two fey-women.

'Why did you take nothing in payment?' said Ysabelon, before he turned away. 'From those ladies before.'

'Nothing?' echoed he in surprise. 'Why, nonsense! Paid me very well, they did.' And he withdrew the twig from a pocket in his jerkin, and showed it to Ysabelon with great pride. Indeed, he rubbed a thumb over its roughened surface, as though caressing the shine on a nugget of pure gold.

'I believe I will take a bottle of your wine, after all,' said Ysabelon.

'Aha!' cried the vintner. 'I'll welcome the patronage of so great a lady, I will at that.' He beamed, and, with a deal of self-important bustle, turned to his well-stocked cart and selected for Ysabelon a slender vessel of airy glass, inside which she saw, not the swirl of imprisoned liquid but the faint glow of blue water under clear ice. This he handed to her with a flourish.

Ysabelon took it. The glass felt warm, which surprised her so much she almost dropped it. Nonetheless, at the touch of her fingers, a liberal coating of frost bloomed over the glass, and crept towards the neck.

Another murmur went up from the crowd.

'I reckon it's true, what the snow says,' someone muttered. 'It *is* she.'

Ysabelon's head turned, but no one would meet her eye; she could not tell who had spoken.

'What will you take for your wine, sir?' she said to the vintner.

'From you, lady, nothing at all,' he said grandly.

This did not suit Ysabelon's curiosity at all. 'No, no,' she murmured graciously, and, sweeping up a handful of twinkling snow, presented this to him as though it were a pouchful of gold.

The vintner all but prostrated himself with gratitude. 'I thank you, lady!' he cried, stuffing the snow into his pockets. ''Tis a good thing that you're come back, that it is!'

'Come back?' said Ysabelon, with a frown. 'Am I indeed?'

'Why, you've been gone a long while, but not so long as all that, surely.' The vintner guffawed, and elbowed his neighbour; a laugh went up among several others, too.

Ysabelon looked from face to mirthful face, and gave it up. None of these folk seemed minded to make any sense; she would seek elsewhere for answers. So, with a stately bow (the occasion seemed to call for it, for some reason), she gathered up her skirts and her frost-flurries and moved on, farther down the river, while the wind howled in her wake.

Everywhere she looked on that strange journey, she saw the same thing: the Frost Fair went on and on, its market-sellers trading winter's treasures for handfuls of rubbish. Though even the treasures were not all they seemed, she judged; she saw a short, graceful little woman, decked in jewels of ice and snow, and when these sparkling ornaments turned to lumps of stone about her neck she did not seem to notice. Another stout fellow wore a hat of snow-spun silk; Ysabelon blinked, and saw that it was nothing but the lacy skeletons of long-dead leaves stitched up with rough thread.

She took a sip of the wine in her frost-garlanded bottle, and found it to contain cold river-water.

'Here!' said someone suddenly. 'Lady! A trinket for such a beauty. Take it.' Into her hand went something heavy: a large pebble found at the river-side, she judged, by its unlovely contours and its dull grey colour.

'This is a pebble,' said she coolly.

An outraged gasp followed. 'It's nothing such! Don't you know a snow-diamond when you see one?'

The pebble was snatched back; but not before the thing had transformed in Ysabelon's hand, and become a diamond in truth, just as the hawker said: a chunk of something precious, rimed in snow all about its edges, its heart as clear and bright as a star.

The glamour did not fade off the trinket afterwards, either; Ysabelon saw it pressed into the possession of some other passer-by, who traded a dead spider for it, and went away delighted.

Meditatively, Ysabelon searched along the river-bank until she found another such pebble. She picked this up, and took it with her, turning it about in her hands as she walked. The stone turned crystal-clear as before, jacketed in hoarfrost, and Ysabelon wondered.

She wondered still more when, having at length reached what seemed to be the end of the Frost Fair, another odd sight met her eyes. The stalls with their haphazard awnings and jostling customers melted away, leaving a clear expanse of frozen river-water stretching away unimpeded, winding a-slumber among the snow-laden trees. But on one side stood something that was no natural part of this scene: a sleigh.

Fit for a queen, this article, for it ran on bands of silver. Elegantly carved boards rose, ice-white and perfect, above. Snow-diamonds and filigree glittered along its sides, and its seats were covered in cloud-like silks. Harnessed to the front, to draw the pretty thing, was a pair of water-horses all frozen over; champing at their silver bits, they hurled cold river-spray into the air, which froze as it flew, and fell in a glittering rain of ice.

There was a coachman, too.

'At *last*!' said this being, upon spying Ysabelon. 'A mighty long time you've taken about it, too!' He unfolded his long length from the sleigh, having been leaning against its bedecked boards, and adjusted the fit of his ornate tunic. He was a tall fellow, and thin, his face ageless and pale as winter itself. A silver shock of hair, bedewed with frost, matched him perfectly to the seats of his sleigh; a fact Ysabelon wondered if he knew, had perhaps arranged for. Surely, the four of them made a fine sight: sleigh, water-horses and driver.

'I am sorry,' Ysabelon felt bound to say. 'I did not know I was expected.'

The coachman rolled his crystalline eyes. 'Only this *age*,' he grumbled. 'A hundred years at *least*, I should say. Well, get in, get in. No time to lose.'

He assisted Ysabelon to get into the sleigh solicitously enough, though with a burning urgency at odds with the sleepy, slumberous winter-forest about him.

'Where are we to go?' asked Ysabelon, as she settled herself upon the welcome softness of the cloud-limned seat.

This question exasperated him as well, for he made a wordless sound of disgust as he launched himself up onto the driver's perch. 'The Court's waiting,' he said, which she supposed was all the answer she was to receive.

CHAPTER TWO

The sleigh bowled along through the frozen forest, so smoothly Ysabelon might have suspected it of possessing wings, had she not seen with her own eyes that it did not. They flashed past an army of grand old trees at an astonishing speed; the forest blurred in her vision after a time, each new tree much like the last, and nothing meeting her eye to vary the scene.

When at last the coachman gave the order to slow, and brought the sleigh gradually to a halt, Ysabelon looked about with eager eyes, expecting some novelty.

She saw nothing but more craggy old tree-boles, and a thick carpet of wind-drifted snow.

'Well, here we are, then,' said the coachman, having got down from his perch, and come around to assist Ysabelon out of the sleigh. 'They'll be waiting for you, my lady.'

Ysabelon did not move. 'But where are we?'

The coachman smiled, as though this were a jest, and held out his hand. 'Quickly now. They'll not wait much longer.'

'They *who*?' Ysabelon said, growing cross, though she consented to clasp the coachman's proffered hand, and descend from her seat. Somewhere along the way, her plain red gown and woollen cloak had gone, or changed themselves perhaps. Now she wore lengths of fine silk fit for royalty, and a velvet mantle, with jewels. The luxurious garments swished about her legs as she moved, and the wind tugged playfully at the hem. 'I see no one,' she added, looking about herself.

This remark won her only an odd look. The coachman said nothing more, but stood by the side of his sleigh, gazing unresponsively into the distance, like a soldier at attention. Clearly, nothing more was to be got from him.

Ysabelon swept past him. Well, then, if she was not to be helped, she would help herself. What sense was it, that had brought her into this wintry wood, back before she had lost sight of Diggory and Mother Gantry? She had gone where her feet had led her, without thinking twice about it.

She did this now, tracing a path from the magnificent sleigh past the trunks of three snow-drowned trees. There she paused for an instant, for the scene was altering itself before her eyes: the next two mighty trunks wavered, as though underwater. When they steadied again, she saw that they formed an archway between them, a portal of interlaced branches clear as glass, and winter-frosted.

Through this arch she saw nothing of note, merely more forest. But only a fool would trust such an innocuous vision, after all the oddities she'd seen that day.

'Thank you,' she said to the coachman, who

looked round in surprise.

Ysabelon gathered her courage, and swept through the archway without pause.

On the other side, she found the most curious vision yet. The forest remained — nothing, she was now persuaded, would ever free her of these *trees* — but mixed in among them were the walls of a vast hall, with long windows inset, bearing glass that more nearly resembled sheets of ice. Through these she caught a glimpse, here and there, of the clustered dwellings of a village, though she could see no way to reach it.

In between those airy walls, some sort of revelry was afoot, for everywhere she looked she saw long tables laden with sweetmeats and fruit. Aromas of sugar and spices hung heavy upon the air. Richly-dressed people wandered hither and thither with crystal goblets in their hands, or lounged upon low couches.

There was not much joy attending this feast, she thought, for the atmosphere was one of languor.

It took a moment or two for some few of these folk to notice Ysabelon. Looking behind herself, she saw no trace of the archway she'd come through; there had been no fanfare to her entrance, she supposed. She'd just appeared.

She ought not to attract any particular notice. Not now, when the garments she wore matched theirs, nearly enough, and she was as tall and as slender as they. But faces turned her way; conversation died; the folk of the Court (for that is where the coachman has promised to take her) stared.

'I am come to the Court, am I?' Ysabelon asked into the silence, for she was a practical woman, and preferred certainty over surmise.

Someone gave an uncertain little laugh.

Then a page was before her, slightly out of breath, as though the boy had run across half the hall (as well he might have). A wispy youth, he nonetheless made her an energetic bow, the silver embroidery upon his livery twinkling in the clear light. 'Almond tarts for her majesty!' he announced.

A silver tray appeared at Ysabelon's elbow, upon which an array of delicate cream tarts was arranged.

'Almond tarts for her MAJESTY!' someone else roared.

'Her MAJESTY!' echoed another. 'Apple ice-wine for her majesty!'

A goblet joined the tarts upon the tray, a heavy silver thing sumptuously engraved, and steaming in the chill air.

Ysabelon looked around for this discerning queen, and saw no one that fit such a description. But the folk of the feasting-hall were still intent upon *her*.

'Your throne, Majesty,' said a lady nearby, a pallid creature clad all in dusk-rose velvet. 'It awaits you.'

This lady bowed, as did three others near her; wintry-pale, every one of them, and wearing similarly handsome gowns, though the others were draped in ice-blue, pale silver, or snowy white.

They drew back, a little, and then Ysabelon saw the throne in question. Large enough to seat four of her abreast, this imposing thing, and carved from clear ice. Frost-flurries swirled around its base — the same ones that had attended her through the forest, perhaps? — and a cushion, of the same cloud-like stuff she had encountered in the sleigh, reposed upon the seat.

Ysabelon looked from face to face, seeking elucidation. 'You cannot mean that this is for *me*?' she said.

The four ladies exchanged uncertain glances. 'Majesty?' said one.

The tray at her elbow jostled itself, causing the goblet to rattle against the silver. 'Almond tarts for her majesty?' said someone again.

'MARCHPANE for her majesty!' came a fresh cry, together with another tray, upon which a second selection of intricate sweetmeats proffered themselves to her.

'I don't quite—' Ysabelon began.

'Your throne, Majesty?' prompted the lady in rose.

Ysabelon found herself, slowly but inexorably, escorted in the direction of the throne. Even the wind joined in, gusting about her legs, and sending all the layers of her mantle and her gown flying out before her.

'If I could just ask a *question*,' said she, aggrieved, but this was not attended to. Soon enough, she found herself sinking into the cloudish seat, amidst a rush of chilling wind and a brief blizzard of twinkling snow.

The faces of her attendant ladies turned from uncertain to delighted; they took up stations near her, two either side of her throne; and below her, across the wide expanse of hoar-frosted floor, the revellers assembled to stare at her.

The ringing tones of an unseen herald rose above the hubbub.

'May all of Wintertide REJOICE in the return of her gracious MAJESTY! Queen of the Winter Court! August Lady of FROST! Sovereign of SNOW! She who is FOND of almond tarts, the highest lady

Ysabelon, Wintertide Incarnate—'

The herald went on in similar style for some time, but Ysabelon, having blanched as white as winter itself at this mention of her name, heard little more of it.

'Am I, then, this queen?' said she, to the ladies surrounding her.

'Of course you are, Majesty,' said the one in silver, soothingly, as though Ysabelon were a confused child.

'How long we have waited for you!' said the one dressed like the snow. 'The Court simply hasn't been the same without you.'

'In fact, it's been exactly the same,' said the one in blue, rather coldly. 'That's the problem.'

'But now all shall be well,' said the rose-lady, beaming upon Ysabelon.

Ysabelon heard all this with a sinking heart. She had been game enough to follow, when those odd Dreams of hers had led her steps towards the Kottow Tree. For who, after so long and wearying a life as hers, would turn down the offer of adventure? Having earned her bread variously as a Seer (in name at least; in practice more of a fortune-teller); a scribe; and even, during one rather thin season, a washer-woman, she'd had little to leave behind that could cause her much regret. She had even married at one time, an experiment she had never repeated, for while *he* had grown old and died, she had not.

Her Dreams had frequently shown her the ice-bound realm in which she now found herself. But they had *not* warned her of what awaited her once she was in it.

'I am not your queen,' she tried, speaking as firmly as she could. 'I feel certain I would have remembered it, if I was.'

But this protestation found no more favour than her previous attempts; her ladies (Maids of Honour, she supposed, just as the queen possessed, in the world outside) laughed this off.

Most of them did, at any rate. The one in blue regarded her more thoughtfully, and finally said: '*Can* it be that you have forgotten?'

The other three, engaged in some chatter among themselves, fell silent at this.

'Yes,' said Ysabelon. 'I have.'

Below the dais upon which sat her throne, the members of her Court were celebrating in riotous style. Having performed a pavane with unusual vigour, they were now venturing upon a lively galliard. The music, jaunty and ethereal, would have lifted Ysabelon's heart, were it not so weighed down with confusion. How oblivious they were to her plight, celebrating the return of a monarch who had forgotten herself!

'So if you will tell me what's afoot,' continued Ysabelon, 'and why it was I was gone, perhaps, I shall be grateful to you.'

This plea went partially unanswered. 'We must fetch the thaumaturge,' said the blue-clad lady, after some consultation with her sisters. 'He will know how to get her memories back.'

'No, Peronel,' said silver-robes. 'He will throw things at us, as you well know.'

'We *need* him,' insisted Peronel. 'What are we to do with a forgetful queen, otherwise?'

There followed some sighing, after this reflection.

'If you will tell me where to find this fellow,' said Ysabelon, 'I will go myself.'

'Gracious, Majesty, *no,*' said the lady in the rose-coloured gown. 'That would never be seemly.'

'Seemly,' repeated Ysabelon. 'I cannot tell you how unconcerned I am with *seemly.*' And, because she was hungry and the fabled almond-tarts smelled heavenly, she took one, and ate it, and felt immediately refreshed. 'The trays may come with me,' she announced, rising from her throne, and taking a marchpane confectioner's conceit next.

She paused, expectant, and when nobody spoke, she said: 'Well? Time is wasting.'

'I will go with you, Majesty,' said Peronel, with a disgusted look at the other ladies.

'Delightful,' said Ysabelon, politely. 'We shall go at once, if you please.'

Peronel bowed her head, and stepped gracefully away; not out into the motley mess of dancers spread out from wall to wall, but to the rear of the throne, where nobody lingered.

Ysabelon followed, her thoughts busy and her mouth full of sweet marchpane.

'We will attend the throne!' called one of the ladies after them. 'Until you are come back, Majesty!'

Ysabelon acknowledged this with a wave of her goblet, prior to downing a draught of apple ice-wine. All three of the delicacies were perfectly to her taste, which she supposed ought not to surprise her now. Whether she remembered it or not, she had of a certainty been to the Winter Court before.

She might have expected that the search for this mysterious thaumaturge might take some time. So irascible and enigmatic a fellow ought to dwell at the top of some distant tower, or in some underground apartment buried deep below. Even the farthest reaches of the forest would have sufficed.

But Peronel, walking at a fine clip, her shoes making ringing *clop-clop* sounds upon the floor, led her only some ways farther down the length of the seemingly endless half-hall, past the trunks of a few trees marooned in the middle of the Court, and stopped before one particular tree. This appeared more thoroughly winter-bound even than its fellows, its bark so crusted in ice as to appear ice-wrought itself. Ysabelon, tilting up her chin, beheld the vast heights of the tree disappearing into a haze of snow-clouds far above, its boughs spreading out to form some semblance of a ceiling for this forestal hall.

A short way up the trunk, there was inset: a door.

Peronel did not attempt, in her Court finery, to clamber up and knock upon it. Instead, she produced (from thin air) a bell made all of clear crystal, its handle a length of, perhaps, the same wood as this pallid tree. When she shook it, crystalline peals reverberated about the hall, and the tree's branches swayed.

Ysabelon held some private doubts as to whether that door would open. *Could* open, in fact, for the thing was solid ice, even its silvered handle and hinges beheld under a veil of hard-frozen water. And indeed, for a while, nothing happened at all.

'The thaumaturge does not wish to speak to us,' she observed into the ringing silence, after the bell's tolling had died away.

'No such thing,' said Peronel dismissively. 'He will answer the summons.' She said this firmly, and with a mulish expression; Ysabelon collected that if the thaumaturge did not answer, Peronel would climb up there herself — fine shoes or no — and haul him out by his hair. If she could pull summoning-bells out of nowhere, doubtless she could spirit up a hatchet as well, or an axe.

These measures did not prove necessary (slightly to Ysabelon's disappointment), for a pounding began from the other side of the door. The trunk shook; ice splintered, and fell away; and the door swung open with enough force to expel its occupant all in a rush.

'Are you the thaumaturge?' asked Ysabelon of the winded fellow lying at her feet.

He squinted up at her, scowling. 'Oh! So you're back, are you?'

Peronel kicked him. 'Some respect is wanted, Mermadak.'

Mermadak the thaumaturge hauled himself to his feet, and bowed to Ysabelon, still fiercely scowling. His was an odd appearance, for he seemed scarcely older than the page-boy who had first brought Ysabelon her almond tarts, and she had expected some venerable sage of a man. He wore Court attire, like Peronel, and all the rest: a silver-threaded doublet with slashed sleeves, all velvet, and rainwater-coloured hose. His was a trifle shabby, however, and not at all clean. In his dark hair he wore a scattering of rain-droplets, spellbound into inertia: or at least, she must assume it was a conscious choice to take them for ornament, or they must surely have dissipated long since.

'Well, and what is it you want from me?' said this sapling. 'The Queen is back, all's well at the Court, huzzah.' This was spoken sourly, with a resentment Ysabelon did not know how to interpret.

'So *they* say,' said Ysabelon. 'But if I have been here before, I cannot recall it. Perhaps I am not this Queen of yours at all.'

Mermadak subjected her to a hard-eyed stare, a scrutiny she returned with bland disinterest. Then, he grinned. 'Forgotten? Well! And what will you of me? Am I to have the honour of mending this complaint?'

'Yes,' said Peronel firmly. 'If you please, thaumaturge, for there's naught *else* to be mended until you do.'

'Naught else?' echoed Ysabelon. 'And what am *I* expected to mend, pray?'

'Why, the Court!' said Peronel impatiently. ''Tis too long since any one of us has set foot beyond the ice, and the forest beyond all empty this while.' She gestured incomprehensibly, adding, 'I thought it lost forever, 'till just today, when *they* wandered in.'

What Ysabelon had taken for a pair of statues of eccentric design proved, upon inspection, to be a hapless pair of fey-folk, frozen solid, and all covered in rime. 'What have you done here?' she cried, storming over to the unfortunate two. 'This is no way to treat guests! And I do not see why you should have done so, if they are your first visitors this age. They might have shown you the way back into the forest, if that's what you wanted.' And they might show *her* the way, thought, Ysabelon, if she decided that flight may be preferable to lingering.

'Well, they could not,' said Peronel, folding her arms. 'I asked them. And it was not *I* who made sculptures of them; the Court did that. It is welcoming of no one save Winter's folk, as you *will* recall, if this lazy-bones can be pummelled into mending your lost wits.' So saying, she advanced upon Mermadak, one dainty fist raised high, setting him cowering with his hands up.

'No pummelling will be necessary!' he cried. 'I'll mend the Lady Frost, and your interlopers too, if you will it. Provided you leave me in *peace*, Peronel.'

'For how long this time?' she said, lowering her fist. 'Isn't a hundred years long enough?'

'No,' he said, blinking at Ysabelon, and narrowing his eyes. 'What do you recall, milady?' He helped himself to one of her almond-tarts as he spoke, which had her minded to issue a reprimand, save that the tray seemed so gratified by the attention.

'Nothing of this place,' answered she. 'Only a stray Dream, here and there, and I now think those were glimpses of lost memories, not visions of the future. Until this day, I lived well beyond the borders of your lost forest, and came into it by way of a wandering Tree.'

Peronel said, 'A *Tree*? Wandering about, and beyond the forest? Ha!' Her face lit up with delight, or mirth, or both. 'Well accomplished, Merigot! And to think I doubted you!'

'And who is Merigot?' asked Ysabelon.

Peronel waved this question aside. 'I shan't keep explaining. It will be needless to do so, the moment Mermadak does his duty.'

Mermadak eyed her sourly. 'You've waited a hundred years, Peronel. Another hour won't hurt you.'

'Who is to say that's true?' she retorted. '*You* have not spent the ages drifting from wall to wall, bound in cold, and with never a glimpse of aught but ice. You've been asleep.'

'Not all of the time,' muttered Mermadak.

Peronel lifted her foot threateningly.

'Yes, yes,' said the thaumaturge hastily. He

straightened his doublet, rather fussily, and shook out his full sleeves. 'I will return shortly,' he announced, and to Ysabelon's dismay, retreated back into his home in the frosted tree's trunk, and slammed the door hard enough to send a rain of rime drifting down.

This did not appear to trouble Peronel, who stood complacently by with her arms folded.

'He is to return, I suppose?' said Ysabelon.

'If he does not, I shall burn down this tree,' answered Peronel.

'Perhaps he will not expect that you would do such a thing.'

'He certainly will.' Peronel bared her teeth in chilling smile.

Ysabelon fell silent, torn between a feeling that Peronel might make a sturdier monarch than she, and a sense of relief that she had not made any attempt to demonstrate the capacity. Things may have gone rather ill with the folk of the Winter Court, if she had — or perhaps she would have put it in order long before, who could say?

Peronel turned the full weight of her regard upon Ysabelon, a slight tapping of her foot betraying her impatience with the wait. 'And where *have* you been all this time, Majesty, if not in the lost forest?'

'Is that where you imagined me to be?'

'Of a certainty. Where else?'

'The world is far larger than these two forests, you know.'

'They are not *two* forests, but two distinct parts of the same one.'

'Forgive me,' said Ysabelon drily. 'Of course they are.'

Peronel nodded. 'Well, and? Where were you?'

'In different towns, far away. You would not know them; they are of no particular note, save that I was contented enough in one or two of them.'

'How could *you* be contented, outside the Court?'

Ysabelon had no answer. She had been contented enough, or so she had thought. But she had also known a perennial restlessness, season after season, which prevented her from making a true home anywhere. In none of the towns of her memory had she known real peace, or been able to set down the roots of a permanent and comfortable existence.

Perhaps this was why. She wasn't one of those plain, good, comfortable folk. She was a creature of Winter, ice through to her core, and could be happy nowhere outside of her Court.

Strange, when she had never much loved the snow.

'Right,' said the thaumaturge, hurling his door open again with a terrific crash, and barrelling out of the house. He half-tumbled down, landed on both feet before Ysabelon, and presented her with an ornate bottle made of glass… or crystal, or cracked ice? One or several of those, at any rate.

Ysabelon took it, doubtfully. 'I have seen these.'

Mermadak raised his brows.

'At the Frost Fair,' she said. 'Someone gave just such a bottle to me — I had it about me somewhere —' She performed a brief search for the article in question, and finding it gone, dismissed the thought. 'It contained rainwater.'

'This one,' said Mermadak proudly, 'is full of wine.'

'Then I shall be roundly drunk, but I do not see

how that will help me.'

'It is Seeing wine,' said Mermadak, rather huffily. 'You will Dream, vividly, and you won't have to sleep to do it.'

'I see,' said Ysabelon. 'And you rustled this up in just these few minutes, did you?'

'Well, I had the wine already,' Mermadak admitted. 'I've added to it.'

'Added *what* to it?' Ysabelon held the bottle up, and attempted, by squinting her eyes and turning the vessel about, to see through the clouded exterior and examine the contents.

'Better not ask,' Mermadak advised. 'Nothing you'd like to drink, ordinarily. But it won't harm you.'

Ysabelon sighed, and thought with brief regret of her washer-woman years. Hard work, that, but simple, and nobody expected her to pickle her insides with stale rainwater, or wine full of unspeakable things.

But if she did not drink it, what then? She could not retreat; the way back into the lost forest — or the greener, balmier part of it — had been closed for long ages of time, and why should it open again just for her? And even if she *could* get back there, what then? Would the Kottow Tree consent to take her back into the rest of the world, as though nothing had happened?

Would she want it to?

'If I am sick,' she told Mermadak, 'I shall be sure to be horridly so, and all over your shoes.'

The thaumaturge took a prudent step back.

Ysabelon raised up the bottle, set her lips to the chill glass, and drank a long draught. It tasted, to her relief, of apple ice-wine, the same that she had drunk not so long ago. If there were other ingredients in there, they manifested upon her tongue as naught but fleeting hints of oddness: a taste as of dried grass scythed down in the summer; a hint of pastry; something, briefly, meaty.

She drank and drank until the bottle was empty, and this she handed back to Mermadak.

He, warily, hovered, eyeing her with profound distrust. 'Well, and are you going to be sick?' said he.

Ysabelon thought about it. Her stomach thought about it, too, being unused to so large a helping of wine all at once. But it contented itself with an unhappy surge, and then quieted.

'No,' she said, adding with a smile, 'Not *yet*.'

Which was not to say that she felt well; not in the least. Her head began to whirl, and a cool mist floated across her vision.

'Oh,' she said in surprise, sitting down all in a rush. Peronel, and even the thaumaturge, appeared far taller from so ignominious a vantage-point, and Ysabelon blinked up at them in a daze. 'I cannot see your faces,' said she, and then she was elsewhere.

CHAPTER THREE

Ysabelon had no difficulty in recognising the place she was come to. There were the twisting, towering boles of ancient trees grown every which way, their grand old boughs and profusion of leaves shading the ground far below. Some few of them looked as though they might at any moment pull up their roots and, like the Kottow Tree, take a constitutional about the forest. Perhaps they had recently done so, or perhaps they shortly would.

The season had altered. When Ysabelon had walked beneath those old boughs before, with Diggory Stokey and Mother Gantry, the freshness to the air and the new growth all around had heralded the onset of spring. Now, the air was grown heavy and sultry, with a slow, deep heat, a sun-dappled balminess — all told her she was gone into high summer. Bees droned somewhere nearby, dancing from wildflower to wildflower, and — more astonishingly — butterflies covered the trunks of the trees, their outspread wings as wide across as her own face. They were painted all the colours of a jewel-box, only more vivid; these were colours to mesmerise, shimmering with latent magic.

That sense of magic pulsed through the forest-floor, in point of fact, the same bedewed and leaf-strewn earth upon which Ysabelon lay. She felt she could soak it up herself, take it up as though she, too, had roots with which to plumb the depths of the earth.

Though she was not lying on bare earth, or even upon an aging leaf-carpet. Under her, there was cloth: a sumptuous length of it, glimmering silk in all the colours of a summer twilight. The pretty thing was spread there by careful hands, she concluded, for she also had about her a feast of morsels and sweetmeats, almond-tarts and marchpane and apple wine, and much more besides. She reclined there, a queen still, pampered and luxuriant.

Most puzzlingly, she felt at her back the shadow of something which — if she were to shift her position *so*, and exert herself *thus* — might become… wings. *Not* like those of the improbable butterflies, not quite: airier, gauzier, dreamier. There one moment and gone the next, like a breath of wind, or a wisp of mist.

They would bear her, though. Oh, yes! Effortlessly; a mere thought, and she left behind her gold-touched platters and goblets, her carpets of silk. Up high, nothing could impede her, and the whole of the lost forest lay spread beneath her.

The butterflies followed her into the air. Cerise and cerulean; the colours of peaches and pears; gold-and-silver glimmering, they surrounded her in a dazzling cloud, and bore her higher still.

They broke through the canopy eventually,

Ysabelon and her bewinged entourage. Up there, the skies were celestial-blue, broken once in a while with wafts and drifts of breezy clouds. Ysabelon felt like a cloud herself, weightless, sailing hither and thither upon the wind. Below her, the forest made an ocean of rustling green.

But then came she to another space, where the viridian tapestry abruptly stopped; emerald and apple-bright and clover and jade all melted away, and in their place came a scene she more nearly recognised: leafless and bare, barren and pale, and the soft summer winds were turned brutally cold.

Down she drifted, too intrigued to mind the blast of freezing winds upon her bare arms and feet. No leafy canopy impeded her progress below. Her butterflies wafted away, one by one, and when her toes touched the fallen snow she was alone.

Winter reigned in profound silence. Ysabelon stepped softly through the snow-drifts, curious, and troubled, for it was not the way of Winter to hijack the summer so. What did it want with this part of the forest?

What did *she* want, more rightly, for around the fat and sprawling trunk of a winter-bared tree Ysabelon beheld another person. Age-bowed was she, her hair cobweb-fine and decked in rime. She wore the winter wind for a mantle, and a half-frozen river tossed behind her eyes.

'Why, Mother Winter,' said Ysabelon, stopping still. 'Whatever is the matter?'

For the crone was in no good spirits, sitting alone upon a jutting rock, and staring glumly at the twisted gnarls of her toes. She looked up as Ysabelon approached, and blinked; a stirring of frost followed the movement. 'Well, and would not *you* be weary, were you the Queen of Winter?' said she, the syllables bone-dry, and windy. She lifted one knotted hand, and gestured at the distant Summer, tantalisingly adjacent to her frozen world. Ysabelon could still smell the verdure from where she stood, the warm breeze still a memory upon her skin. 'I wanted to step in,' continued Mother Winter. 'Just for a moment! But it won't wait for me.'

Ysabelon beheld the effects of Mother Winter's efforts: the trees here had been decked in Summer finery not long since, she thought, and somewhere under the sudden-fallen snow there waited a carpet of green. 'Winter goes where you go, Mother,' said Ysabelon. 'That is the way of things, is not it?'

Mother Winter answered only with a sigh, a long exhalation, and in it Ysabelon heard the distant howling of a gale.

The memory of Summer receded, moment by moment; Ysabelon's bared arms prickled with the cold. What might it be like, indeed, to be bound in Winter forever? Never to know the warmth of strong sunshine, the scent of fresh verdure in your nose, the light, tickling touch of a butterfly alighting upon your skin?

'It must be a trial to you, Mother,' said Ysabelon, moved to pity the old lady. 'What if you were to have a holiday? Just for a little while?'

'How could I do that?' demanded Winter, fixing Ysabelon with her ice-water stare. 'Who's to mind the Winter while I am gone?'

'Well,' said Ysabelon, and thought. 'I could do it, could I not?'

'You?' said Mother Winter, dry as dust.

'I am a Summer queen already,' Ysabelon confided. 'I am sure I could care for Winter, for a space.'

In another moment, she might have taken back the words, if she could, for she did not like the smile that came to Mother Winter's face. Merciless, she thought. Cruel and cold, and why should that surprise her, when she held Winter itself in conversation?

'I shall be obliged to you,' said the crone. 'I wouldn't want to entrust it to anyone less than a queen. But I am sure *you* could do it.'

'I could,' said Ysabelon firmly, but was she convincing the hag of Winter, or herself?

'How long a space?' asked the Winter. 'Don't be mean-spirited, now! I have never had a holiday before, and you, being a queen, will hardly notice my poor Winter in your train.'

The ice-water eyes twinkled, and Ysabelon did not like that, either. But it was too late to retract, now; *she* could not be so cruel.

She thought.

'Until my brother comes for me,' she decided. 'He went walking, not so long ago. He won't be back for some time yet.'

Mother Winter smiled.

'Mind you don't think to impede him!' Ysabelon said, having bethought herself of an obstacle. 'He must return when he wills it, and without any interference of yours.'

'Done,' said Mother Winter. 'When you should clasp hands once more with this brother of yours, I shall take back my Winter, and consider myself much the better for a rest. Is it agreed?'

'It is,' said Ysabelon.

Mother Winter's smile grew. 'I am grateful,' she said.

The burden of Winter settled over Ysabelon like — like — a mantle thrown abruptly over her shoulders, its enveloping folds hiding everything else that she was. If a mantle could weigh as much as a craggy mountainside, that is, and if it could be as cold as a glacier. Ysabelon staggered under it, her shoulders bowing, and as the ice penetrated her heart she began to shiver.

'You will get used to it,' said Mother Winter, straightening even as Ysabelon crumbled, and stretching out a figure grown youthful and lithe. 'In a little while!'

Then she was gone, darting into Summer with a single leap, leaving Ysabelon alone in the snow.

When Ysabelon, Queen of Winter, began, with tottering steps, to drag herself to her Court, the bleak and barren cold went with her. Gusts of snow roared in her wake; frost-flurries danced around her feet; and everywhere she looked, Summer withered under the blizzard of her gaze.

And though she waited and watched day by day, her brother never did return. The frost could not find him; the snow could not reach him; wherever he was gone, neither Ysabelon, nor any of her Winter-bound subjects, could follow.

'Well!' thought Ysabelon, somewhere at the back of her waking mind, remembering. 'Of all the shabby tricks to play! Why, the crone has been gone for a hundred years, at least!'

As had she; for the whirl of memories did not wait for her to unravel her thoughts about Mother

Winter's perfidy. She saw herself, ice-bound, returning to the Summertide Court; and of course, her arrival changed it utterly. Her beasts and birds slunk away; her Trees dropped all of their leaves, and sank into slumber; her lords and ladies grew cool and chill, and wore snowflakes in their hair.

She went to the river, and wished that she had not, for it froze over at her approach. A Summer market was in full swing, up and down its banks, but all the fine produce sank under rime; vendors and fair-goers alike withered where they stood, turned as mean and cold as the lords and ladies of her Court. They swindled each other mercilessly, trading old twigs and spider's webs for treasures equally spurious; and no expostulation of Ysabelon's could change them. The longer she remained, the icier they grew, until she ran away in despair.

And so Winter's Queen sat once again alone, her heart heavy, all her hopes dwindled into sorrow. The worst of it was, she could not wholly blame the crone for her trickery; for would not she herself give *anything* to be liberated from this punishing existence? And she had borne it for only a span of days!

She thought of her woodlands, where her Court gathered in the Summer; where the glimmerlings swarmed thickly over the trunks of the trees, spreading their bejewelled wings wide. Where, when the clouds massed themselves up and burst gloriously open, the deep magic of the forest mingled with the water, and rained enchantment upon those below.

Thinking of these things, the mystical and the commonplace alike, Ysabelon wept. Her tears froze as they fell, became a flurry of clear diamonds plummeting into the deep snow.

'*Fool* of a brother!' cried she. '*Where did you go?*'

A voice came from the air, tolling like a great bell. 'Would you like to know?'

Ysabelon thought she detected the frozen strains of the Winter-crone, hidden somewhere within those sounds. '*You!*' she cried. 'Come back at once! You have destroyed *everything*.'

'Would you like to know?' repeated the voice. 'You might go to him, if you wished it.'

'Of course I wish it,' grumbled Ysabelon, rising from the rock upon which she had seated herself. She saw nothing of the crone, nor anything else that might explain the voice; all was barren Winter. 'I'd clasp his hand at once, and you may take this burden back.'

The crone was smiling, wherever she was. Ysabelon could not see it, but she *felt* it, felt it in the prickling of her skin.

Before her there stood a particularly tall and mighty Tree. The dry bark of its trunk splintered and cracked; a door opened.

'Step in,' said the voice. 'And off you'll go.'

Ysabelon peered cautiously inside, fearing some fresh trick of the crone's. But she saw a comfortable space, furnished to withstand the cold, with a quantity of blankets and rugs and what-not.

She paused to think. Doubtless the crone intended some further mischief. But the facts remained: if Ysabelon did *not* find what had become of her brother, she would remain the Winter-Queen for all of time.

'I will go,' said she aloud. 'Upon one condition: Winter stays here. I will not drag it about with me.'

'Done,' said the voice, in a ringing way, as of a

binding spell.

Ysabelon went into the Tree. The door closed behind her, and at once it began to walk; the simple chamber within dipped and swayed about in a most disconcerting fashion, but Ysabelon hardly noticed. The Winter was draining from her limbs, from the very core of her.

By the time the Tree had walked some little distance away from the Winterwood, Ysabelon stood tall and strong, more herself than she had been in days.

When the Tree gathered itself and began to run, she clung to the furniture; uselessly, in the end, for it *leaped*, sending Ysabelon tumbling to the ground.

When later she woke, it was to a fierce headache. The Tree was gone, not that she would then have recalled it. She lay near a stone-built fountain in a simple market square; she'd been asleep, to all appearances, though it was not like *her* to drop where she stood, and make a common beggar-woman of herself. She rose hastily to her feet, avoiding the gaze of a pair of village-children who'd stood in fascinated scrutiny of this spectacle, and went about her business.

Elsewhere in the town, the man Gower Bordekin packed up his peddler's wares and trudged away into the fields. He passed within a few feet of Ysabelon, but they knew each other not.

His path would not cross Ysabelon's again for many a long age of man.

PART FOUR

THE SUMMER COURT

CHAPTER ONE

Gower Bordekin, whisked away out of the lost forest like his sister, was gone into Summer. So said Maut Fey, with her Summer-seeing eyes, and she spoke accurately.

Not that Gower noticed the burning heat that had so impressed Maut. He strode through the cinnamon-coloured forest with unimpaired energy, the cream-and-honey petals settling on his shoulders and his hair, and breathed in the aromas of home.

The dappled emerald light pleased him; he knew it for his own, even if he did not remember why. Not yet would he recall the lady lost to Winter, his own sister Ysabelon. Not yet would he remember the role he himself had once used to play in these parts. For now, he remained Gower Bordekin the blacksmith, the peddler. The sometime wizard of the Kottow Tree.

For a while he walked on alone, and though a bird or two rustled in the boughs over his head, or floated through the gold-lit canopy above him, he encountered nothing else living. His heart untroubled, he wandered on, for some part of *this* he had seen, in his lingerings in the mists at the top of the Tree. He had waited twenty-one years to set foot in this Summer-lit forest, and he was in no hurry to leave it again now.

It occurred to him that the quantity of birds about him was increasing. He saw some of the same bright creatures keeping pace with him above; as gold as the light, these, with long, sweeping tails, and here and there a startling glimpse of riotous colour. Others joined them, until the Kottow Tree's wizard (or blacksmith) had a fine, feathered entourage gathered in his wake. What they were doing there, he couldn't have said, being unfamiliar with their beak-clacking, cackling speech, but he didn't mind them.

Then he came to a break in the endless march of the trees: a wide clearing, the centre of which had something in it. A nest, though made of nothing so mundane as twigs or grass. The thing was bright-gold, spun from shimmering heat itself, he thought, and in it lay a dragon all curled up asleep.

'Good day,' said Gower, stopping, and taking in the scene with interested eyes. The dragon looked ancient indeed, as though some of the colour had gone out of him; what was left was a faded and dulled bronze. The creature didn't stir.

'Good day!' Gower called again, more loudly. 'I say, sir, are you quite well?'

One eye opened. The dragon was no diminutive beast, being at least twenty times Gower's size, and the topaz eye must be the size of a dinner plate. Somewhat filmed with rheum, this eye, and sluggish.

The dragon's only response to Gower's polite

enquiry was a waft of steam spun from one nostril.

'Do you need anything?' Gower persevered. 'You don't look altogether well, if you'll forgive my saying so.'

'It is too hot,' breathed the dragon, wheezily. 'It has been too hot all these long ages through.'

The eye closed.

Gower looked about himself. Hot it might be, but not dry, for nothing withered; rain came often enough, then. But the shimmer in the air: was that a glimmer of magic, or merely intense heat? Both, mayhap.

'Is there nowhere cooler you can go?' Gower said.

Another puff of steam: a feeble laugh.

Gower took this for a negative. 'Hm,' he uttered. 'Perhaps if your nest were made from rain instead, or better still, ice?'

'The rain never lingers,' wheezed the dragon. 'And what manner of ice could do so?'

Gower thought about it. 'Perhaps it might, if I asked it to,' he offered.

The eye opened again. 'Oh? And who are you?'

A bird cackled overhead.

'Nonsense,' said the dragon, the eye narrowing. 'Not this paltry fellow?'

'I hardly know who I am,' said Gower, wondering. 'But I feel different here, than I did out there.'

'Out where?' asked the dragon, but Gower disregarded this, being engaged in an experiment. He felt powerful in this heat-blasted forest, in ways he had never quite felt before. Maybe he *could* conjure ice up out of nothing, if he tried.

He made the attempt, and found it simple: the dragon's nest shone still, but with a white-cold light, and Gower felt the chill of it even from some distance away.

'It won't linger,' said the dragon with a sigh.

'It will,' said Gower. 'As long as you would like it to.'

The dragon only sighed again, and closed his eyes, and Gower walked on.

He encountered next a family of phoenixes, sunset-feathered, and wreathed in a nimbus of heat. These were not woeful, like the dragon: they relished the fiery climate, and when he came upon them he found them sailing through the trees, turning like kites upon wafts of heat-shimmer.

'Good day!' he called cheerfully, and one of them turned its firelit eyes upon him.

Gower found himself studied, in momentary silence.

'I would say as you're the queen,' said the phoenix. 'You've her aura. But you are not she, are you?'

Gower looked down at himself, found himself reassuringly man-shaped, as always. 'I am not,' he called back. 'To my knowledge. Surely I'd know, if I'd become queenly.'

'Then you are a rival.'

'Hardly.'

'She won't be pleased.'

'I have no wish to be anybody's rival,' said Gower, certain of the truth of it as he spoke; only afterwards did he pause, and think: who *was* this queen? Was this not *his* forest-home?

'She'll want to see you,' said the phoenix.

'Why?'

'She likes curiosities.' The phoenix considered the conversation finished, for the bird took to wing again, and soared away.

Gower was left to ponder the meaning of these unpromising, yet intriguing words. Did he want to see the queen? Perhaps. He was interested, now.

'Where do I find this lady?' he shouted after the firebirds, but they did not return, and nobody spoke to him again.

'Well, then,' said Gower with a shrug, and wandered on. His feet had always got him where he needed to go, before; now should be no different.

'It is that way,' whispered the softest of voices, from somewhere in the vicinity of his left knee.

He looked down.

He strode through a tangle of undergrowth, most of it creeping low to the ground, and not much impeding his steps. Little of green was there to be seen; much of it tawny and gold, this growth, heat-blasted shades, though with a thirsty beauty of their own. Gower noticed blossoms of grand size, with glossy trumpets for petals, and curling stamens; and underneath them, blossoms in miniature, star-shaped, perhaps, or like tiny crowns.

Poised in the centre of the grander sort, dwarfed only by the sheer size of its chosen abode, sat a bejewelled insect, its proportions near exactly matching those of Gower's clenched fist. This being had a shining carapace of amber-gold, dusted with something that glittered. The fine ladies whose handmaidens visited the Kottow markets, buying bolts of the best cloth for finery, would not have scorned to wear that shining carapace for a necklace.

'Did you speak?' enquired Gower, nonplussed.

'I did,' whispered the beetle. 'If you want to see the queen, it is this way.' And the beetle took to wing, darting off from flower to flower in swift spurts of energy, trusting to Gower to follow.

Which he did, being possessed of a powerful curiosity about this jealous queen, the one who feared every possible rival to her power. No secure lady, then, nor any wise ruler either, if the state of her kingdom were anything to go by. It had beauty without mercy, this place that baked all the joy even out of a wily old dragon.

The beetle led the blacksmith through a wide meadow rustling with a fair crop of some wheat-like stuff, a whole tapestry of it in honey colours. They journeyed on through a copse of trees, the spindly kind, tall and bending in the breeze, not the firm-planted behemoths of before. They passed over a river of rushing, frothing waters, sputtering with golden foam, and went up and then down the slopes of a hill grown over with prickling grass and aureate clover.

At length, Gower's limbs wearied, and his breath came harshly in his throat.

'Are we like to be there before year's end?' he called to the beetle. 'This queen of yours seems a long way off.'

The beetle stopped, alighted upon a tall thistle-thing, standing proud of a field of low-growing verdure. 'She is no easy being to find,' said the beetle, peevishly, its wings *flick-flicking* in irritation.

'I apologise,' said Gower. 'I meant no reproach.'

The beetle settled. 'Perhaps you are right, at that,' it said next. 'Chasing about the place like this, it's humiliating.'

Gower's brows rose.

'If the queen wants to talk to you, she will,' and

away flew the beetle without another word, leaving Gower standing up to his calves in frondy grass, stranded.

He paused a while in thought, disconcerted. How touchy a creature! Though he had been ungracious, which was not like him; perhaps the heat was getting to him after all. 'Come back?' he called. 'I shan't complain anymore.'

But the beetle did not return, and nobody else spoke to him, either.

So Gower trudged on a while, going in much the same direction as the beetle had been leading him, and waited for something to materialise.

As so often happens with some longed-for thing, time seemed to creep by, as though it had nothing better to do than saunter along, enjoying the weather. Gower's searching eyes swept the horizon, again and again, hoping every moment to catch a glimpse of something that augured the presence of a queen. A castle, mayhap, its turrets flying bright flags, and hung with pennons. A carriage bowling along, conveying the elusive monarch on some expedition of pleasure.

Nothing emerged. All that happened was that a quantity of clouds drifted over the sun, obscuring the strong sunlight, and in due course of time a pattering of raindrops came down.

Gower sighed, for the depth and heaviness of those thunderous clouds heralded the onset of a storm. He'd be soaked to the skin in minutes, and so he was; bathed in a rain that was, somehow, as hot as the air around it, the droplets sizzling as they struck his skin. No cooling interlude, this.

And it had a curious effect on the landscape about him. Under the deluge of heated rain, odd colours washed over the verdure about him, green included (as one might expect), but many another hue besides. Even Gower was not spared this treatment, for under the rain-flow his own skin altered, shifting in hue, darkening and then lightening by turns, and his clothes underwent several fleeting transformations. What began as simple, workaday attire ran the gamut from peasant's rags to a king's finery, and back again.

To his discomfort, when the maelstrom lessened, a mere few minutes after it had begun, Gower's garments did not return to their original state. He was obliged to wander on, dressed in a doublet whose velvet folds and rich embroidery would not have disgraced a prince; his legs were encased in cobweb-fine hose; and a soft weight about his brow announced the acquisition of a hat, a soft velvet cap by the feel of the thing.

Stranger still, as the clouds boiled off again and the rain ceased, leaving a drenched and glistening world behind it, Gower sensed the weight of somebody's approval, as though either the rain or its mischief had pleased some powerful being beyond sight.

'All right, then,' he shouted, and spun in a circle, showing himself off in all his borrowed raiment. 'If this pleases you better, Majesty, then show yourself.'

A rumble of thunder answered him, puzzlingly, for the storm-clouds had fallen into tatters and streamed away. The sky returned, piercingly blue, and all a-shimmer.

'Well?' Gower barked. 'I haven't got all day, even if you might.'

'Of a certain, you do,' came a sultry voice, from nowhere. 'All day, and all year. All your life, if it pleases me.'

Gower pursed his lips. 'Of a certain, nay,' he decided. 'That wouldn't suit me at all.'

'And why should I mind what suits you?'

Adjusting the sitting of his hat, Gower drew himself up to all his mighty height, and smiled the smile which had weakened the knees of more than one honest lady. 'Why, because this is *my* home,' he called. 'If you displease me too much, I'll make a rival of myself in truth.'

The boiling heat made short work of the fallen rain, however drenching the quantity; the air filled with warm billows of steam, and when it cleared, everything was bone-dry, Gower included.

'A rival,' mused the queen, her words echoing from all about him. 'How long it has been, since I had one of those!'

'Well, try it now,' said Gower, all affability.

'I wonder if it *would* amuse me,' pondered the queen.

'Oh, thoroughly! And I shan't at all mind obliging you, being as I'm none too well pleased just at present.' In illustration of this point, he tugged impatiently at one sleeve of his sumptuous doublet, and kicked at nothing much with the toe of one jewelled shoe.

'What, don't you like what I've done for you?' gasped the queen. 'But I have showered you in riches!'

'Is that what that was? A shower of riches? For my part, I'll have none of it.'

The approval in the air turned to a pouting resentment. 'Whyever not? Riches suit you, far better than that musty claptrap you had on before.'

'But it isn't mine.'

'Mayhap it is. You might have forgotten.'

Gower took a moment to think on this. The lady was right: he had forgotten a deal of things. He knew that he had, felt it as yawning spaces in his thoughts. A collection of impulses, half-felt, none of them understood, the reasons for which lay hidden behind some veil, some haze, in his imagination.

Nonetheless.

'That's as maybe,' he called. 'But if I don't remember it, I don't want it.'

'What if I could make you remember?' The words were dulcet-sweet, coaxing.

'You would like that, would you?'

'I don't like your ingratitude.'

'Oh, I'm to be grateful!' Gower's chest swelled with an indignant breath. Truly, he ought to have been on the stage, among the many lives he'd had. 'For borrowed finery! Jewels that don't belong to me! You've dressed me up like a puppet, Majesty, and for your own amusement, not mine.'

'But you do look so well in it.' Sweeter still, these words, like a fall of honey.

'Now, there's to be no hoaxing and coaxing of me,' said Gower. 'If there is aught you want me to recall, make it so. Otherwise, I'll be on my way.'

'Come and see me,' said the queen, her voice like the dry rustling of wind in tall grass. 'I would look upon you.'

'You are already doing so, not?' said Gower.

'I would have you look upon *me*.'

Gower gave a great, windy sigh, and took a step. 'Very well. Where am I to go, then?'

'Yonder.' And there, directly ahead of him, rose the very castle he had looked in vain for, not long

134

ago, though the construct was of a strange kind. Half castle, half forest, if the mixing-up of walls and tree-boles was to be believed. Had the castle grown over the forest, or had the forest grown over the castle?

Gower turned his steps that way, guided by the airy snap of sun-lit streamers flying from the distant tops of towers. They seemed a long way off still, these spires, so he was surprised indeed when a mere half-dozen steps brought him into a courtyard, paved in light, with tall walls of yellow stone jostling for space with venerable old oaks.

'You could have done that any time these past hours, could not you?' said Gower, planting his feet in the middle of that courtyard, and consenting to move not a step farther in. 'I suppose it amused you to have me plodding like a donkey through your kingdom.'

'In fact, it did.' The voice came still from the air around him, but it seemed nearer now, as though the lady herself might be hidden behind the trunk of a nearby tree, or tucked into a nook in those stout walls.

'Very well, you've had your fun.' Gower looked about himself, alert for a glimpse of golden hair (for he doubted not that the queen of these sunlands must match her kingdom in that). 'Come out, now.'

She did. Gower's ears picked up a rustle of fabric, and the dry, sweeping sound a long train makes as it drags over dry earth and crisp leaves knocked down by the wind.

Then came into view the queen herself, the fingers of one outstretched hand trailing fondly over the rough bark of a hoary oak. A great beauty, she, which surprised him not at all: was not her kingdom all beauty, all over, down to the meanest twig, the tiniest leaf? So bright and golden as to hurt the eyes, after a time, and so was the lady: gold hair all down to her ankles, eyes beryl-bright, and skin the same smooth, cream-and-golden hue as the petals that whirled in the winds of her kingdom. She wore finery to put even his borrowed plumage to shame: a gown of shimmering silk, or something like, jewels winking at cuffs and neckline and hem, and with that lengthy train he'd heard trailing behind her.

'Well?' said the queen, lifting one brow, and gazing at him with a challenge in her glorious eyes. 'And are you pleased with your monarch?'

She spoke with the supreme confidence of a woman well assured of her own beauty, and accustomed to unalloyed praise.

Gower looked her over critically.

'Well, and I might be,' he decided. 'If I weren't fair certain that these beauties are no more your own than this fine, fancy suit belongs to me.'

The queen drew herself up, all the sunshine draining out of her face. 'Do you call me false?'

'Well? Aren't you?'

A flicker of doubt crossed that perfect face, followed by anger. 'You won't like remembering,' she warned. 'You swagger *now,* but you'll stop soon enough.'

'Shall we find out?' said Gower, pleasantly. 'I'll take the consequences, if I dislike the results.'

A wave of cold hit him, incongruous indeed in the midst of hitherto unbroken heat. It came from the queen, and for an instant there was nothing of high Summer about her at all. She was ice to her core, and not the beauteous sort either. A killing cold, the implacable fury of winter wind.

'Ahh,' said Gower softly, beginning to see.

This only enraged Her Majesty more. She stooped, and swept up a rock, fallen from somewhere. This, childishly, she hurled in Gower's direction. It smote him upon the brow; he felt a warm trickle of blood follow.

'Aye, 'tis relieving to the feelings to throw things,' Gower agreed. 'But—'

He stopped, his thoughts lost in a sudden confusion.

The queen gave a wolf's smile. 'Enjoy your remembering,' said she. 'You see, all this could be construed as *your fault*.'

Gower, falling into the misted past, could not answer her. But the sickening feeling in his gut suggested that, in this at least, the queen might well be right.

CHAPTER TWO

It is not the way of memory to arrange itself, neatly, into events of chronological order. It required conscious effort, later, for Gower to wrestle the messy mass of recollections into something like a story.

There'd been a certain night, once upon a midsummer many years ago, when Gower had made the fateful decision that exiled him from the forest. But it hadn't started there.

It had begun a day or two before that night, with the courtier known as Plumwood.

Plumwood was a clever fellow, bright and swift, quick of wit — and overflowing with mischief, though seldom did he direct any of this at his liege lord-and-lady. Whether it was mischief that led him to Gower's side that lustrous morning, or some other impulse, the Summer Court's king could not have said; not even now, with the benefit of hindsight to assist him.

The night hours belonged to his sister; Gower was a creature of morning and afternoon, of a hot sun soaring through an azure sky, of clear air shimmering with heat and magic. Plumwood found him at high noon, halfway up a towering cedar, with his broad back resting against the broader trunk and his face turned up to the sky. Some one or two of the fiery birds he loved had joined him upon the bough and sat there dozing, their long, vibrant tails sweeping low.

'Majesty,' hissed Plumwood from a branch below, crouched there like a squirrel or some such thing, and dipped his head as Gower looked down. All tall and thin today, he resembled a bundle of sticks loosely collected, and dressed in moth-lace and tangle-vine. Plumwood loved the rain, and *would* stand out in it, whenever the clouds burst open; as such, he never looked quite the same way twice, when Gower encountered him.

'What is it?' Gower called down, having opened his eyes only briefly, and soon closed them again. The sun's warmth on his face had sent him half into a dream, and he was loath to wake from it just yet. But Plumwood took to dancing upon the boughs, or so it felt, and the wind joined him; the rocking of the branches soon opened Gower's eyes again, and brought him frowning down upon the fey beneath.

'Majesty, I have found it,' said Plumwood, holding up a twig with a single, silvery leaf clinging to one end. 'I have found a Way.'

'A Way where?' said Gower, unimpressed.

'A Way *out*,' hissed Plumwood. 'Come, and I'll show you.'

Out? Out of the forest, did he mean? Gower

would have asked, but that Plumwood had already dashed off, like a squirrel again; all he lacked was a bushy puff of tail to lash about as he moved. Halfway to the ground already, there was no stopping him now. Gower must decide whether to humour him or not.

Curiosity bit at him. If Plumwood had found a Way out, *all* the way out, why, that was news indeed. With a sigh, then, Gower let the winds form at his back, and wove a set of wings from sunlight-gauze. A mere thought carried him into the air, and there was Plumwood below, hastening over the forest floor.

Gower had taken the wayward courtier's wings a while, for some forgotten offence. He gave them back now, out of impatience if not mercy, and with a crow of delight Plumwood jumped into the air and joined his liege-lord in the skies.

Progress was faster, after that, though the journey to Plumwood's find took longer than Gower preferred. Still, time passed, as it will, and delivered the Summer Court's king and his courtier to a quiet glade in some distant, dusty nook, a forgotten corner of the fey-forest where scarcely anything dwelt.

Lying prone across this mossy glade was a fallen tree, silver-clad, with pale leaves all a-flutter. The thing was not dead, somehow, for living branches erupted still from the downed trunk, and unfurled leafy streamers in the air. A carpet of moss had grown over the bark.

'Well, and what of this?' said Gower, planting both feet into the cushion of moss, and inspecting the fallen thing. ''Tis but a Tree, Plumwood.'

'Aye, but where do its roots go?' said Plumwood, gesturing.

Gower descended from the trunk, and followed the fey's pointing fingers. The roots went a long way, as it happened, a fine thicket of winding wood running all out into the moss. Gower walked with them, placing his feet with care, and found the Way. Tucked between two fall, frothy ferns was a pocket of mist, swirling gently there, quite as though it had every right to loiter in such a spot. The roots went into it.

Gower walked around it, and to the other side: the roots did not come out again.

'Do you see?' said Plumwood. 'The roots have gone right through the mist, and into Somewhere Else.'

'Where else?' said Gower.

Plumwood gave a shrug, and sat sunning himself upon the fallen bole, beaming in satisfaction with his own achievement. 'I'll go and find out, if you will it so, Majesty.'

'But you haven't yet.'

'I haven't.'

Gower thought the matter over, though not for very long. 'I'll not send you through,' he decided. 'Who knows but what you might be gone a long time, and I couldn't spare you. I'll send someone else, sometime.'

He had not *then* an overpowering interest in this door in the mist, for he was (as he told himself) perfectly happy in his Summer-limned forest. What need had he for a Way Out?

But curiosity had got at him, and though he turned his thoughts and his steps elsewhere, it did not wholly let go.

A little later, then, under the moon this time: the Lady's hours. Gower sat with his sister in her favourite glade, one she had, with her own fair hands, decked in perfumed flowers. Petals shone silver-bright under the moon's distant glow, tangling all across the moss-carpet, and twining up the trunks of the Lady's slender birch grove. In the midst of all this glory the Lady lay reclining, her handmaidens having laid out a feast for her, and a silken couch from which to enjoy it.

Gower attended her. He might not have done so, had the matter been entirely by his own choice. But while *he* lorded over the day, when the moon rose the tables were turned; Ysabelon was Queen, and Gower stood at her right hand. If she wanted him about her, then he would obey.

Tonight, she did, though not for any purpose Gower could determine. She lay contented, a crystal goblet in one hand (filled with a silvery wine), the fingers of her other wreathed in moon-beams. *He* sat restlessly toying with a fallen birch twig, glancing up, now and then, at the cool, lunar beauty which so entranced Ysabelon, and wondering.

His thoughts turned upon the fallen tree, its roots off in some distant place. What *did* lie beyond the mist? He had not given the matter much thought at the time, but no sooner had he turned his back upon the scene and walked away, well, he could think of little else.

He had never been Outside the forest. To wander off was no part of his duty; his kingdom needed him. The fey-creatures of the sunlit wood could not be left to shift for themselves, with no liege-lord to defend them. If he did that, how long might the balance of day and night remain in their proper order? Given half a chance, his sister would steal half the sunshine away, and replace it with moonglow.

He would do the same to her, given half a chance. It was their way.

No denizen of his realm or hers had ever gone Outside either, of that he was fairly certain. But rarely was there the means to do so. Outside the forest was not for them. Inside, under the velvet canopy and the moss-hung vines, with the clear air in the throat and the soft ferns underfoot — *there* was safety, and beauty, and home.

But...

Who was to say what lay beyond? No one knew. Mayhap it would not be a danger at all — or if it was, nothing that the King of Summer could not master.

Mayhap, somewhere beyond, there lay a land where the sun never set at all.

Gower shivered at the mere thought of it. And once *that* idea had got into his head, there was no getting it out again.

And so, on that tranquil, fateful eventide, he abruptly stood, letting the birch-twigs fall from his hands. 'I shall go for a walk,' he announced to his sister.

Ysabelon glanced up at him in faint surprise, though the silvery wine had already mellowed her too far for alarm. 'Very well,' said she, smiling. 'I shall see you anon.'

'Anon!' he agreed, beaming, and then he was gone, striding energetically away from the perfumed bower. A leap carried him into the skies, and from there he did not pause until he'd found Plumwood's glade again.

No more did he hesitate, once he espied the mist-shrouded Way Out. He dove through all in a rush, a single, deep breath drawing the cool moon-mist down into his lungs.

And that was the last that he recalled of Gowerlon Summer-King, though he did not know what it was he had lost. Many a long year would pass before he would find his way back, or Ysabelon either (though that *she* might also be lost in the World Beyond would not have entered his thoughts, even had he remembered her name).

All this passed through his mind, as he lay insensate at the heat-baked Court of the trumpery creature who called herself the Summer Queen. When he came to himself, and cleared the fog of a hundred years' rememberings out of his thoughts, he was left with a fierce anger, the kind that made an inferno out of his guts, and set his head to pounding. But not all of it could be directed at the usurper.

'That is what *you* have done, is it not?' he snapped, his gaze moving from the golden lady's face up into the burning sky above. 'You've done away with night. It is naught but sun all the time, now, and while I'll not deny it's a thing I have coveted my own self, clearly it doesn't answer.'

'What does the Summer want with night?' answered the false queen. 'Leave the dark and the cold to Winter. We've no use for it *here*.'

'Winter?' echoed Gowerlon. 'And you know it well, do you?'

In answer, he received only a strange smile, an odd curling of the lips which did not reach the lady's eyes. Those eyes, he thought, turned hard as frozen water, somewhere behind their golden glimmer.

'And who are *you*?' he said, sitting up. 'I've a head full of answers, but none of them tells me how *you* came to take my place in the forest. If I'd had to guess, I'd have said it would be Summer-Night eternal, now, and Ysabelon Moon-Queen reigning over the lot.'

'Ahh,' said she, her smile turning cruel. 'Yes. What *could* have become of her, I wonder?'

'You had something to do with it,' said Gowerlon, rising to his feet, though the blood rushed in his brains and he swayed, in unkingly fashion, like a sapling in a storm. 'I would bet my kingdom on that.'

'But you've no kingdom to lose, do you?' said the queen.

Gowerlon pointed one implacable finger at the lady's lovely face. 'The forest has not forgotten me,' he said. 'Yours are borrowed feathers, madam, and I will have them back of you.'

'Will you so?'

'Aye.' Gowerlon drew himself up, the pulsing in his head ebbing away, and leaving him stronger by the moment. 'This,' he went on, waving an arm at the forest-palace around him, 'is not all of the forest, is it? You could not take it all, or you could not hold it — I've no interest which it was. Only this miserable pocket belongs to you, and it'd thank me to be rid of you, I'll be bound.'

He fancied that the lady turned a shade paler at his words, but her composure held: she did not flinch.

Something in her at that moment, though… it put him in mind of another thing. Mayhap it was the glacier that lurked, deep and cold, behind her eyes; or mayhap it was only some flicker of intuition, a sense of Gowerlon's own possessing.

Summer and Winter had not often had cause to talk to one another. Once, though, in some distant past, had Gowerlon Summer-King's path crossed with that of his polar opposite.

'Mother Winter,' he said softly, taking a step nearer. 'Is that you?'

Now that composure faltered. The lady took a small step back. She stopped there, held, and lifted her chin; but Gowerlon had seen.

'Grown weary of the cold, is that it?' he said, advancing upon her. 'Had enough of ice-bound rivers and snowdrifts?'

'Would not *you*?' snapped Mother Winter.

'Well.' Gowerlon stopped, set his clenched fists upon his hips, and stared Winter down. 'You've had a good, long holiday, have not you? Now it's time to go home. Let me have my crown back, Mother — and let out my sister, from wherever it is you've put her. It is time to restore order in these parts.'

'You'll not have it back.' Abandoning all her honey-sweet cajolery, Mother Winter spake the words with Winter's own, merciless spirit.

'Return it, and my sister and I shall show clemency,' said Gowerlon, through gritted teeth. 'We'll offer no punishment. You can return into your Winterlands unharmed.'

'I will not.' Old Mother Winter straightened, thin as a reed, and in another moment she was gone. Where a queen had stood, there remained only a glitter in the air — a glitter of sunlight on ice.

Her voice echoed from the air around the displaced Summer-King. 'Keep what's left of your forest, Summer Lord, if you will. But this part is *mine*.'

She was gone in truth, after that; Gowerlon felt

her absence, as one feels the emptiness in a long-abandoned house the moment one steps over the threshold.

'Ran away, is it?' he mused, pondering. She was not so confident of her strength as she'd have him believe, then.

But that in no way assisted him in the immediate moment. He did not know precisely what she had done to wrest this part of the forest from the Summer. How would he go about getting it back again?

His thoughts turned to the others. Those he'd travelled with, from the World Beyond: Mother Gantry, and Mudleaf, and Diggory and Maut Fey. And those he had left behind, much longer ago than that.

'Well,' he said to the air, and took a breath. 'I wonder what has become of Plumwood?'

CHAPTER THREE

What had become of Plumwood, Gowerlon was not yet to discover, for the forest bore no traces of his recent passage.

He wandered for some time, attempting to discover the usurper-queen; and when that failed, to locate some member of his long-ago Court. But Mother Winter had frightened them all away, or she'd locked them somewhere, mayhap the same fate as had befallen Ysabelon Moon-Queen. A near-desert she had made of his forest, heat-blasted, empty of life and laughter.

How she could take any pleasure in such an accomplishment, Gowerlon had no power of understanding. Weary of Winter was she, or so she said, but she had made a Winter out of Summer. It was only a glossier vision of the season: better-lit and brighter-coloured, but half dead.

Mayhap she knew no better. What else would Winter make out of Summer?

Such thoughts attended Gowerlon Summer-King's disconsolate wanderings out of the Summer Palace again, and back through the glittering forest beyond. His steps trailed past the phoenixes' nests, and ended at last in the dragon's glade.

He found there an altered creature since his last visit.

'Ah!' cried the dragon, with an alacrity he had not had the energy for, a little while ago. Both of his topaz eyes opened, and fixed the Summer-King with a searching stare. 'AH!' he called again, and this second utterance was more of a shout. 'You've grown,' he added, in a milder fashion.

'I've remembered a few things,' said Gowerlon.

'I should say you have.' The dragon sat up in a rush; drew himself straight up, his wings flying high, and spat out a gout of celebratory flame. 'I thank you for the ice,' he chattered, toothily beaming. 'That was a kindness.'

'It was my pleasure,' Gowerlon assured him. 'I trust you're feeling restored.'

'A fair way so. Your having vanquished the queen, now, that helps a deal more. And you did it so promptly, too! That's a real King of the Court.'

'But I haven't.'

The dragon settled down on his haunches, his festival of flames dying away. 'No? What a pity that is.'

'I shall,' Gowerlon promised. 'As soon as I find a way.'

'Why, surely it cannot be difficult,' protested the dragon. 'She's only a usurper.'

'Yes, but she's been at it a while,' Gowerlon explained. 'The forest has not forgotten me, but it's tried.'

'It has been a long time,' said the dragon, disapproving.

'I'd forgotten myself,' Gowerlon apologised. 'I didn't mean to.'

The dragon produced a thoughtful puff of smoke. 'Not everyone has forgotten you.'

'Everyone? I have scarcely seen a soul. Haven't, in fact, save for you and the queen, and the phoenixes yonder.'

The next waft of smoke had the air of annoyance about it. Indeed, the dragon gave a snort of pure disgust. 'Foolishness does not become the true monarch of Summer-Morn,' he said, and severely, too!

Gowerlon felt a flicker of irritation. 'What have I said that's so foolish?'

'Nothing at all, I'm sure! Doubtless the feathered flocks have some sound reason of their own to follow you all the forest through.'

Startled, Gowerlon looked up into the overhanging boughs. They were still there, indeed: a fair number of coloured birds in myriad hues, gazing down at him with gleaming-black eyes.

'Mayhap they admire your figure,' said the dragon, dulcet.

An idea entered the Summer-King's head. 'Plumwood?' he called.

Nothing stirred overhead.

'Brackenberry?' he tried, which was productive of nothing, either. 'Mudling? Barleythorn? Willow-Wild? Quince?'

Here a better result, and there also: the names Barleythorn and Quince brought a pair of feather-fey fluttering down.

'Made birds of you all, has she?' said Gowerlon, his ire rising again. 'Or was it the rain that's done the mischief?'

'Mayhap both,' said the dragon. 'The rain's not been in order this long while.'

'Aye, nothing has,' sighed Gowerlon. 'Well then,' he called up to the feathered flock. 'What will you? Fey or feather?'

He held out both hands as he spoke, permitting his lost Courtiers the choice.

They took it. Two elegant, plumed heads bowed low in obeisance; and when Barleythorn and Quince rose, they'd shed their feathers, traded tails for wings, and stood tall(ish) and fey again.

Barleythorn shook his dumpy little self all over, like a bird bathing in water, and grinned as he made another bow. 'My thanks, Summer-King.'

'Aye!' echoed Quince, testing her jade-coloured wings; she spun a circle in the air, shedding white petals every which way. 'I'd not like to remain a bird for all my days, that I can tell you for certain.'

'Welcome back Quince, and Barleythorn,' said Gowerlon, hiding some of the buoyant delight he felt, for a king ought to have some dignity. 'It does my eyes good to see you.'

They radiated back such joy that Gowerlon forgot his dignity, and began to laugh. There, that was more of Gower Bordekin; the man may have been a Dream, but one he'd not like to forget, all told.

'Delightful,' murmured the dragon behind them, observing their brief horse-play with a tolerantly satirical eye.

Quince darted off, and tweaked the scaled tail for it. 'Come, Nynlath, I'll see you dance before I'm gone!'

'Never,' said Nynlath the dragon coolly.

'Never, is it?' Quince booted him in the rear, gently enough, but a firm strike; the dragon twitched.

'When the queen's overthrown, then I'll dance,' Nynlath amended, snapping his large jaws in Quince's direction.

'From dawn until dusk,' said Quince. 'We'll look forward to it, old one.'

'Yes, and how are we to arrive at this happy event?' Gowerlon interposed. 'Come Quince, come Barleythorn. Tell me what I've missed. How was my kingdom wrested from me? And what's become of Plumwood, and Mudling, and Willow-Wild?'

'All gone after you, Summer-King,' said Barleythorn. 'Gone all these ages, and never returned. What, are they not with you? Mauvian either?'

'No,' said Gowerlon, and thought. 'Not to my knowledge, at least — nor, perhaps, to theirs. We'll see. But the queen, now? Tell me of her.'

'In truth, Lord, I think it took no special might,' said Barleythorn. '*You* were gone, and the Moon-Queen also. Who was here to gainsay the Winter?'

'*We* tried,' amended Quince, lightly kicking Barleythorn. 'Not that it availed us much. Feathered in a trice, were we, and brainless feather-guts we've stayed, 'til now.'

'My honour on you for the attempt,' said Gowerlon, with a courtly bow.

Barleythorn and Quince returned this gesture with glee, and topped it off with a dance.

Nynlath's response to this malarkey was another snort, and somehow or other the hem of Quince's dress caught a spark, and lit up.

'Oh!' cried she, beating out the new-born flame in a hurry. 'Wicked!'

'Assault not the rear quarters of dragons,' said Nynlath, 'and you'll not be scorched.'

Quince stuck out her tongue, and awarded him a fine view of her turned back, and the indignant set of her shoulders.

'*So,*' persevered the Summer-King. 'What say you, then? We take the Winter Queen out of the way, and all's well? Can that be all?'

'All?' echoed Barleythorn, squinting. 'It's enough, I trow.'

'First, we'll find my sister-queen,' Gowerlon decided. 'I'd like her might with mine, when we challenge the Winter.'

Quince and Barleythorn, interpreting this as an order, bowed in unison. 'Sire!' said Quince.

'And what of the rest of my Court?' mused Gowerlon. 'Gone after me, you said.'

'Long since, Majesty.'

'I've a notion where they are.'

'Not with you, you said?' enquired Barleythorn.

'No, but I've a notion they *were*. That Tree! A wily plant, and patient enough for six. Quince, or Barleythorn, tell me: how shall I get out of this Summer-adust place, and back into *my* part of the forest?'

'Out past the borders?' said Barleythorn, exchanging a glance with Quince. 'No one's gone in or out, Sire, not this long while.'

'The Winter's doing?'

'The Forest's doing, methinks,' said Barleythorn. 'Winter wanted it all, but she never got it.'

Like severing a diseased limb, Gowerlon thought, in order to protect the trunk. Sense enough. And mayhap that was how he'd come into this section of the wood in the first place: the Forest had brought him, and might return him, too, if he asked it the right way.

'Nynlath,' said Gowerlon. 'Do you stay or go?'

The dragon shuffled his wings, thinking. 'What will become of my nest, if I go?'

'Was it so handsome a specimen as all that? You'll not need the ice, out beyond.'

'Ahh,' said Nynlath. 'Beyond. And what will we do *there*, Summer-King?'

'If we've luck on our side,' said Gowerlon, smiling, 'we'll find Mudling and Willow-Wild, and Brackenberry, and Mauvian Lovegood. Mayhap Plumwood, too, though I've less certainty of him. And then, fellows all, we'll find what's become of the Moon's Queen.'

'You've need of me, have you, King of the Summer?' Nynlath spake the words lazily, and with doubt, or mayhap it was derision.

'Likely I will,' said Gowerlon. 'And I'll not *like* to go alone. Who would do so, that had a choice of company?'

'Always *was* a carousing sort of fellow,' snorted Nynlath, but he got out of his nest, stretched out his wings, and sauntered over to his liege-lord. 'Very well then, take me on this fool's errand of yours. I've a liking for some entertainment.'

'Your confidence overpowers me,' said Gowerlon gravely.

'You'll not have company *and* confidence of me,' said Nynlath. 'It's of no use to wish for it.'

'I'll take the former, then, and be glad of it. Well! We poor few, away into the Forest we go.'

He did not wait for any more chatter, nor courtesies either, but caught the wind as it passed, and wafted away on it. Quince and Barleythorn would follow, he knew, and Nynlath — as it pleased him.

To the edge of the Winter's demesne, he asked of the wind: *carry me there, and quickly.*

The wind bore him swiftly through the dry, moss-bare boles; over the searing yellow of the dandelion meadows; round Winter's so-called Summer Court, half claimed by the Forest, but unsubdued; and delivered him at last to the foot of a veritable wall of verdure, interspaced at intervals with ancient, sere trunks, and woven between with a tangled thorn-thicket taller than Gowerlon. He could picture Winter's attempts to pass this barrier: with what vicious glee the thorns would tear at her soft flesh! With what violent pleasure would the hoary copper-beech wind its branches through her hair, its roots around her limbs, and pull, pull...

The vision, somewhat bloodthirsty, took him aback, and he paused. 'Am I remembered?' he called, softly, for if the Forest here had taken so against *one* monarch, would it welcome another?

Nothing answered him, but nothing attempted a wild destruction of his person, either, and he took *that* for encouragement.

'I'd like to pass,' he announced. 'With my Court, what's left of it: Quince and Barleythorn, and the dragon Nynlath.'

A rustling went up, of crisp, dry leaves rattling in a

rising wind: a sound with a trace of menace threaded through it.

'I'll come back for the Winter,' he promised. 'A reckoning between us lies ahead. But my Court lies behind me, and my sister, mayhap, and I have need of them.'

The rustling grew, but it was not leaves now, or not all of it. It was the thorns unwinding themselves, and parting, making a gateway under the wine-red eaves.

Gowerlon darted through it at once, certain the gap would close before long. Who knew but that the Winter-Queen might find a way through it, and make an advance on the Forest beyond? 'Swiftly, Quince and Barleythorn!' he called. 'Pick up your feet, and follow!'

Nynlath needed no encouragement: the dragon spread his wings, the size of Kottow's market-hall, and wafted over the barricade. Not a single thorn attempted to prevent him.

Gowerlon had taken the gateway at a run, and he went on running, with a hasty thanks uttered to the forest behind him. His feet remembered the earth here, now, his nose the scent of every leaf and petal; the moss-growth underfoot, the damp mud and the clear air; everything spoke, painfully and joyfully, of *home*. Gower Bordekin had known nothing of it, but Gowerlon Summer-King — *he* knew every tuft of grass, every fern, every ivy-vine and wild rose.

His mad and joyous flight ended in a tumble, landing Summer's Sire full-length in a patch of fragrant fern-leaves. There he lay laughing, for a little while, as Quince and Barleythorn pelted him with withy-twigs, and the forest itself sent a rain of apple-blossom drifting down over him.

Then up he sat, abruptly. 'Now, then. To business. We must find Mauvian, first among everything.'

'Why she?' said Barleythorn, sitting cross-legged at Gowerlon's right hand.

'She's wise,' said Gower, tucking a spray of blossom into his hair. 'And I've a notion her way with the smaller beasts may be of use to us.' Squirrels, he knew, went everywhere, saw everything. If anyone could tell where Mudling and Willow-Wild had gone, not to mention Brackenberry and Plumwood, and maybe his sister too, mayhap it'd be they.

'Nynlath!' he called up to the skies, for a large shadow was passing over. 'What do your dragon-eyes see? Have you a glimpse of others under the boughs?'

The dragon did not answer at once, but the shadow circled about, blotting out the glow of the sun once or twice, and then came there an almighty crashing and splintering: a grand beast landing itself among woodly obstructions, none too gracefully.

Then came Nynlath's voice: 'I've a sense of somebody.'

'Is it Mauvian?' called Gowerlon. 'A lady-fey, that one, with the sun behind her eyes, and a whiff of fur about her.'

'It isn't she.'

'Alas. Who, then?'

'I might say as it's the one you call Plumwood,' said Nynlath. 'I met him, long ago. I think I'd remember the scent.'

'Oh?' Gowerlon sprang up, and made for Nynlath at a dead run. 'Plumwood!' he called, raising his voice over the clamour of the wind. 'Plumwood, come to me!'

'He won't hear you,' said Nynlath, his voice rather nearer.

'Come, is he a bird now, too? I've a remedy for that.'

'Not a bird.'

Gowerlon found Nynlath sunning himself in a bit of a clearing, at the centre of which lay the rippling waters of a sun-dappled pool. Embedded in the earth near the shore of this water-way was a craggy lump of dark granite; lounging with his haunches upon a cushion of moss atop it, was a squirrel.

This squirrel had fur the colour of... well, of plums, thought Gowerlon, enlightened.

'Plumwood,' quoth he, falling to his knees beside the creature. 'What a state you're in.'

The squirrel — or Plumwood, if it was he — consumed a beech nut with deliberate care, spitting out the husk in a spray of small pieces.

'You don't know me,' said Gowerlon, dismayed. 'Quince? Barleythorn? Shall you try?'

They did, and with no more result. The squirrel went on with his dinner, at least until Nynlath, impatient, snapped his jaws near to one quivering ear, and the squirrel went three feet up with a squawk.

'Right,' said Gowerlon. 'He's coming along with us, either way,' and he scooped up the chattering beast. The creature quieted under his touch, contenting himself with a few last, choice insults hurled at the dragon, and on the little party went.

'You're certain it's Plumwood?' whispered Quince, drawing near.

'Fairly,' said Gowerlon. 'For all that Plumwood alters with the rain, the one thing that doesn't is the hue of his hair.'

Quince looked doubtful.

'Why, you've some other reason in mind as to why a squirrel might be so fruity a shade?'

'The rain alters many things, Sire.'

'But not by turning them purple. I'll have Mauvian's opinion of this fellow before I will give him up.'

'And where are we to find Mauvian?' asked Quince, not without cause. 'It's a wide forest.'

'And somewhere in it is one particular Tree, taller even than those you see about you, and it's got a fondness for me. Also for Mauvian. Nynlath will spot it, before we are many hours older.'

The Summer-King spoke truly, though the search took longer than he would have liked; by the time the dragon aloft sounded the Tree-alert, and trumpeted the news below, the sun had wandered all across the heavens, and begun to sink. Not so poor in timing, thought Gower, for when better to seek the Moon's Queen but under the moon's glow? He witnessed the slow rising of this heavenly body with satisfaction, and welcomed the gentle, silvering tint of the shadows as it came.

'Summer Lord, if I were not afeared of seeming mad-brained, I might say as your Tree is walking about,' shouted Nynlath from somewhere above, all trace of his passage indistinguishable now, with no sun's rays for him to get in the way off. How the dragon could fly so silently, him being so immense, came as a mystery to Gowerlon.

'Then it's the Tree that we want,' answered he. 'Leastwise, if it isn't raining.' He held up both hands, palms upward, to test for falling droplets, and found none.

Nynlath's silent progress ended in another clamour of landing, and breaking of branches, and crashing of large bodies through dense canopies.

'Grace to match his manners, that one,' said Barleythorn, sour.

'But wings and eyes to meet our needs, and other senses too,' said Gower. 'Without him, we'd not have found Plumwood here, nor the Kottow Tree either.'

Barleythorn acknowledged this with a nod.

'It is that way, yonder,' came Nynlath's voice, and, turning in the direction of the dry syllables, Gowerlon beheld a flicker of lambency through the darkening trees: a lantern hung on the Kottow Tree, mayhap the one beside Diggory Stokey's door.

He went forward to meet it, Quince and Barleythorn at his back. Their Tree ambled slowly along, like it was out for a pleasure-stroll, and perhaps it was. Glancing up, Gowerlon saw nobody balanced upon the boughs, and looking down; if anyone was aboard, they were inside, behind the tight-shut doors.

'Ahoy!' he called merrily, his heart lifting at the sight. 'The Kottow Tree! Anyone in?'

He repeated this cry a time or two more, before anybody heard. But *then*, Mother Gantry's door came crashing open, and a face looked out. Diggory Stokey's. His mouth fell open, upon beholding who had hailed the Tree, and as his gaze travelled from Gowerlon to Quince and Barleythorn, he found nothing to say.

'Well, Diggory Stokey?' came Mother Gantry's voice. 'Who is it, then?'

'Why, I'd say as it's Gower,' said Diggory, collecting his wits. 'Only I ain't rightly sure of it.'

Mother Gantry's face appeared, peeping out from

behind Diggory. Her eyes narrowed.

'Is Maut with you?' Gowerlon called, waving. 'I've a powerful need to have speech with her.'

'Let me through, then, Diggory,' said Maut, and appeared at the door, though not quite as he'd *last* seen her. More as he'd *first* seen her.

'Mauvian!' he cried, beaming. 'I thought as it'd be you.'

'Is that my name? Well, mayhap it is,' Maut allowed, or Mauvian; the two names mixed themselves up in Gower's head, or Gowerlon's: nothing made all that much sense, at present.

'Which do you want me to use?' he asked.

'Aye, that's sense there,' agreed Mother Gantry.

'A body can choose her own name, to be sure,' said Maut, or Mauvian. 'And that being the case, I've always liked Jesmond. But to have *three* names all to myself must be a mite greedy, and confusing to boot, so I'll remain Maut.'

'Maut, then,' said Gowerlon. 'I—'

'And what has become of *you*?' she interrupted, looking him over, with much the same look on her face as had touched Diggory's.

'You don't yet remember?'

'Vaguely.' Maut squinted at him, lips pursed. 'I've a dim memory only, at least since the rain. You're an important fellow, are you not?'

Quince and Barleythorn had hitherto listened to this exchange in silence, but now spoke up.

'His *Majesty* ought to win more respect!' pronounced Barleythorn. 'It's customary to greet the Summer-King with a bow, *thus*.' And he demonstrated, with superb grace, his courtliest obeisance, while Quince curtsied low beside him.

'The Forest's liege-lord, he,' added Quince, tartly, 'in case you've forgotten.'

'*I* never knew him for a monarch,' said Diggory. 'Nor Mother either, I'll be bound.'

Quince looked him over. 'No, for you *are* mortal, aren't you? Mauvian, what do you want with these?'

'It's Maut, now,' came the answer, 'whatever I might have been before. Quince.'

'You remember me!' said the fey, clapping.

'And Barleythorn. Aye, I do. The rain's leaked in through my ears, perhaps, and got to my brain.' She did not choose to bow to Gowerlon, or Gower, but her eyes strayed back to his face, and beheld him in a moment's quiet, and then she inclined her head. 'Summer-King. I did not know who I spoke to, all those long afternoons up the Tree.'

'Nor did I,' said the fey king, 'but I'm Gower still, Maut.'

That won him a smile, and some of the trouble faded from her amber-washed eyes. 'Well, and what was it you wanted to say to me?'

He produced Plumwood, and offered the squirrel up to her. 'We've need of your beast-friends, in a little while. And what do you make of this fellow?'

Maut stepped down out of the Tree, and when both feet were planted on solid earth she held out her hands, and accepted the small form of Plumwood. Her face changed at once. 'What, not a squirrel? But he looks the part.'

'I believe him to be your own fellow Courtier, Plumwood.'

Maut's lips formed the name, silently, and with gentle fingers she stroked the soft, plum-coloured fur. 'What's done this to him?'

'The Winter, methinks, though I'm not certain. Can you change him out of the enchantment?'

'If you cannot, I am sure I am helpless,' said she.

'Mayhap he likes the shape,' came Nynlath's dry voice from the shadows.

'I've a dragon with me,' Gower explained, when the three Tree-dwellers looked up. 'Nynlath. He found the Tree.'

'A pleasure, Nynlath,' said Maut, her eyes fruitlessly scanning the shadows. She'd not see him, not in so deep a twilight.

'A dragon as well,' sighed Mother Gantry. 'What next.'

Diggory put an arm about her shoulders in comfort. 'Steady now, Mother. All shall be well.'

'Can we borrow your furred friends?' Gowerlon pursued. 'My sister's a hundred years lost somewhere in the forest — in Winter or Summer, mayhap, or some other part — and I must find her.'

'Your sister.' Maut looked oddly at him, her head tilted. 'The Lady.'

'The lady?' repeated Diggory, alerted. 'What, the lady Ysabelon?'

'What!' uttered Gowerlon, striding forward. 'You've seen her, then?'

'Naturally we have,' said Mother Gantry, and she had an odd look, too, as she stared at him.

A smile was playing about Maut's lips. 'Gower, surely you couldn't have been so oblivious?'

'I'm known to be, on occasion,' he admitted. 'Tell me, then: what have I missed?'

'She isn't a hundred years lost,' said Maut. 'A few hours, belike.'

Gowerlon stared.

'The lady as boarded the Tree, when it stopped,' said Mother Gantry. 'Didst thou never clap eyes on her?'

'Or hear her name, either,' said Maut, eyes brimful of laughter now.

'No,' said Gowerlon slowly. 'I made a hermit of myself, did I not? And hid at the top of the Tree. And when I came down, near everyone was gone, except you.'

'Well, that was the lady Ysabelon,' said Maut. 'Your lady sister, I gather.'

'But,' said Gowerlon slowly, thoughts awhirl. 'How came she to be on the Tree? How came she to be outside the forest?'

Maut shrugged. 'How came any of us to go Beyond? Doubtless there's a tale, and we'll hear it someday.'

'She's not above?' asked Gowerlon, with a searching glance up at the darkened boughs, as though he might see the Moon-Queen seated there, laughing at his foolishness.

'No, she's lost these few hours,' said Diggory. 'Vanished, like you did.'

Gowerlon cursed. 'We came out of Summer to find her, and left her behind us, did we?'

'No, no,' said Diggory. '*She* went somewhere far colder than that.'

'She's at the Winter Court, I suppose,' said Maut. 'Though what she is doing there, I couldn't guess.'

Gowerlon thought. Winter's own queen had gone into Summer, and stayed there; now the Summer Queen, the Moon's Lady, had gone into Winter in her stead. 'Is everything topsy-turvy in these parts?' he complained.

'Near enough,' said Maut. 'What shall we do? She'll want to be fetched out, I'll wager.'

'Mayhap,' said Gowerlon. 'Though I don't know as she is bound. If I got out of the Summer, she can come out of the Winter, surely.'

'Then she's engaged in something of a purpose,' said Maut. 'Mayhap she'd like help.'

'Aye. Can your squirrels find the way in, think you?'

'To Winter? I'll ask them.'

'Ask them to seek the Winter Court, or the Summer Queen; she may be returned already.'

Maut nodded. 'And what then, if we find her?'

'We've a visit to pay upon Old Mother Winter.'

PART FIVE

TIB

Let us go back a ways in time, until before the sun had set on the lost forest (a few hours, no more). We're to find what's become of that wily and wiry young fellow, Tib Brackenbury. Among the first to venture down from the Kottow Tree, from almost the moment it stopped, Tib had enjoyed both time and vigour enough to cover a lot of ground. He had Berengaria Dow along with him, for the two being of similar disposition in many ways (merry of temperament, energetic of body, and adventurous of spirit), they made a natural cohort.

All had gone along charmingly, for a time; a jaunt through an enchanted forest under a midsummer sun must please anybody not very much given to gloom, and these two were in a state of high glee.

'Oh, look, Tib, look!' frequently cried Berengaria, pointing out some fresh wonder to her companion (be it one of the pretty white squirrels that flocked to Maut's knee, perhaps, or a blushing glade of blossoms, or even a glimpse of those long-tailed birds that had so entranced Willow Wildboots).

Tib was not so responsive to this flow of admiration as she could wish, for his was a more avaricious character (and he had the light fingers to go along with it). Less moved by a show of beauty, Tib's bright eyes kept a keen watch for anything precious. Because of this, his journey through the forest pleased him a mite less than Berengaria's, but he was an optimistic man, and made the best of it.

So passed the first two or three hours of this lively team's wanderings beneath the boughs.

Then came the rain.

It passed over them in a swift shower, so swift it might have fallen from the swollen mass of a single, fast-moving cloud (which, mayhap, it did). The wash of colour and life that it coaxed from the forest delighted Berengaria, naturally. Tib may have been disappointed that the magical stuff did not make jewels of the stones under his feet, say, or gold leaf of the verdure.

'Aye, pretty enough,' said he, beholding, at Berengaria's insistence, a violet-winged butterfly, somewhat oversized. 'But I cannot take it with me, can I now?'

'Do you think of naught else?' chided Berengaria, less moved than usual to charm this particular young man. He was short, and plain, and she had no eyes for his homely countenance.

'What else is there to benefit me?' retorted he. 'A

man must think of the state of his pockets, or they'll lie fallow for all his days.'

'Fallow pockets hasn't ever harmed *me* very much.'

'I daresay, but you've looks to secure *your* comforts, and I, milady, have none.'

Berengaria could not quarrel with this conviction, not even to please a friend. 'Very well, have it as you choose,' said she tartly. 'Though if you must fix your thoughts on riches, and I upon beauty, methinks I've the best of that bargain today.'

'For now,' said Tib. 'If one thaumaturgical shower brings gigantic winged critters in its wake, who's to say what the next one might offer? It'll be gold, or something like, I'm sure of it.'

Since Tib Brackenbury had the kind of confidence, and unabashed swagger, that made his every assertion sound like truth, Berengaria did not oppose such a belief either.

'I'll even share, when it comes,' added he, generously. 'For all that you doubt me.'

'Aye, for naturally, else-wise, every scrap would belong to you.'

'Naturally!'

So much for the confident expectations of Tib Brackenbury. But the rain brought no gold to weigh down his draughty pockets, nor jewels to adorn Berengaria's fair hair either.

What it brought, to begin with, was confusion.

'Tib!' said Berengaria, a preface, doubtless, to some new, glittering discovery.

But Tib said, with a frown, 'No. That isn't my name.'

'What can you mean?' said Berengaria, laughingly, too little of her attention fixed upon her companion to see the trouble in his face. 'Tib, look, surely that's a glimmer of gold over yonder.'

It wasn't, but that made no matter: Tib barely heard her. 'It isn't my name,' he insisted. 'I can't think how I came to be known by such a syllable. Why *do* you call me that?'

'It's how you are known,' said Berengaria promptly. 'And you told me so yourself, when first we met.'

Stubbornly, Tib shook his head. 'I can't have — or I was mad at the time. The name isn't mine.'

Berengaria sighed. 'Well then, what shall I call you?'

'It's Brackenberry.'

'You've a distaste for one part of your name, but not the other, have you? I think it odd, Tib — Brackenbury — but very well.'

'Bracken*berry*,' he said.

'Brackenberry.' Berengaria, losing interest, wandered off after a passing butterfly.

'We'd better hurry,' called Brackenberry after her. 'Or we'll never find the king in time for Mother Gantry's tea party.'

That caused an immediate halt; Berengaria stopped, and turned. '*What*?' she cried. '*Have* you lost your wits?'

Brackenberry stood blinking, as though something in his line of vision — or passing behind his eyes, mayhap — caused him pain. 'No, that isn't right,' he said, more softly, addressing his own thoughts rather than Berengaria's words. 'The king? Where did I get that idea?' He attempted to laugh it off, but the sound lacked his customary mirth, and ended sooner.

'Is Mother holding a party?' asked Berengaria,

falling into step beside him, this time, when he started off again. 'I hadn't heard it.'

'Isn't she?' Brackenberry sighed, and fell silent a while. 'It's no use,' he said, somewhat later. 'I *will* keep thinking of the king.'

'What king?'

'The King of the Summer, though only in the daytime. When the moon rises, those are the queen's hours.'

'A queen as well, is there?' Berengaria looked upon the erstwhile Tib with some concern. 'The rain's addled your wits, I fear, though it doesn't seem to have altered mine.'

'Addled?' said Brackenberry. 'Or something else? Beren, I think I *know* these woods.' He turned all in a circle, seeking something familiar, and seeing plenty. 'That stump, there — the knotted one, with the rain pooled in the top. I remember the tree it used to be: a mighty oak, and once we held a midsummer night's feast right under it. The queen, and all her Court were there, and the king, too.'

'Tib—'

'It's *Brackenberry,*' he snarled. 'The king gave me that name himself, when he appointed me to his Court, and I'll bear it still, though he may be gone.'

Berengaria permitted herself a small sigh. 'Very well, Brackenberry. And where has this king gone to?'

'I've forgotten,' said he, despairingly. 'Did I find him, or not?'

'Why don't we ask the queen?' said Berengaria, with a flippancy Brackenberry might have thought unbecoming, if he'd noticed it.

In fact, the teasing suggestion caught, and held him; he looked up at the darkening blue glimmers of sky, glimpsed between sprays of green. 'The queen! Yes!' he cried. 'The sun's going down, I do believe; she'll be feasting, soon.'

'Oh, to be a queen! Nothing to do but feast under the moon, and hold Court. I believe I should like it very well.'

Brackenberry ignored this, too. 'Leave me if you choose,' said he, 'or come along, but I'm away. The queen's bower is not so very far from here, and she may yet remember me.'

By no means displeased by so enchanting a prospect as a queen's woodland bower, and a feast on a moonlit night, Berengaria elected to go — even if all the sense had washed out of her friend.

Away went Brackenberry, Berengaria following. That the man seemed to know just where to put his feet, and what winding path to take through the darkening trees, did not admit of a doubt. Never did he pause, or even hesitate, and though the route seemed longer, to Berengaria's weary feet, than he had promised, he strode confidently on.

As they went, the last of the sun's weakening rays swept over the forest, and died. Enthralled, at first, with the delicate silver glint of a cooler light setting the forest aglow, Berengaria went along very happily. But shadows crept in, and deepened, where the moonlight could not go; and she wondered how it was that Brackenberry, or Tib (as she must still think of him, protest though he might) could march on, untouched by confusion, though he could see but little of his path. Not his eyes, but some other sense, led him onward to the queen's bower.

'You did say it was not far?' called Berengaria at last, for her throat was dry with thirst and a growing hunger clutched at her insides. She thought, with regret, of Mother Gantry's tea-party, that existed only in Brackenberry's addled head.

'Impatient girl!' cried he, though not in anger. He spoke in high merriment, his spirits buoyant, his steps jaunty with expectation. 'Don't despair, fair Berengaria, for it's just around the corner.'

Berengaria might doubt the truth of this assertion, but she ought not, for Brackenberry did not lie. Around the hulking silhouette of yet another grand tree went they, and there stood an arch: a woven portal of cherry-tree, and tangled jasmine-bloom. Through it went Brackenberry, without pause, and Berengaria followed.

A glade lay beyond, a velvet-dark spot, and limned all in moonlight. Heady with fragrance was the air; thick with jasmine and lingering traces of honeysuckle, with phlox and moonflower, and night-scented orchids. A carpet of deep, emerald moss covered the floor, where it was not grown over with flowers, and in the centre, where the moonlight shone strongest, there stood a chair.

A throne, rather, Berengaria thought, going nearer to it, for the thing was taller than she, and a living construct, grown there by the willing contortion of root and branch, and bedecked in night-blossoms. A mossy seat beckoned, but not to Berengaria. Even she, daring a girl though she was, and enchanted by such beauty, would not have presumed to seat herself in it.

Brackenberry blustered in, alight with anticipation. But as Berengaria drifted about the glade, peering into this and that, and filling her lungs with the sweet perfume, Brackenberry stood still as stone, and all the joy went out of him.

'There's no one here,' said he.

'Not a soul,' Berengaria agreed.

Brackenberry lifted his voice, and shouted. 'Hi, Plumwood! Pearl-a-way! Peronel, and Lavendale!'

No one answered, though he waited, without breathing, for some time.

'Briarbud?' he tried. 'Alverin? Merigot!'

'They are gone, I think,' said Berengaria, into the silence. 'Like the king.'

'Yes, but the queen— if *she* is gone as well, then I do not know—' He paused, and looked about him in consternation. 'Then who has cared for the forest? Who has there been, to shepherd the Summer?'

'Where has this king of yours gone?' said Berengaria, her practical side asserting itself. 'Wherever *he* is, mayhap your queen is there also.'

'Out,' said Brackenberry, after a moment's frenzied thought. 'Out! He went beyond the forest's borders, and it was all Plumwood's fault, too. So Plumwood said we ought to go out ourselves, and bring him back, for the king was gone longer than an afternoon, and missed the dawnsong. So we went, some few of us: Mauvian Lovegood, and Mudling, and Willow-Wild.'

His quick brain needed little prompting, after that: the face of Maut Fey rose in his mind, and he gave a shout of delight. 'It's more than just me as has come back, with the Tree! Mudleaf, and Wildboots — close enough, I trow. They're here somewhere.'

'And the king?' said Berengaria, plucking a jasmine flower, and holding it to her nose. In her secret heart, she might be forming designs upon this king, for a queen's verdant throne sat vacant. If nobody else was minded to adopt the role, well, for what else was Berengaria here?

It did not happen that Tib Brackenbury and Gower Bordekin had crossed paths, very often. Gower preferring his station at the top of the tree, and Tib much below, they had not come much in one another's way; and then Tib had enjoyed the company of Berengaria and Diggory Stokey, while Gower delighted more in that of Maut. As such, the befuddled Brackenberry had to think longer and harder than might seem right for a man (or a fey) so lively of wit.

In due time, though, Gower's imposing frame found its way back into his memory, and he wondered.

'Beren,' he said.

'Yes.'

'When the Tree stopped, before we came to this place. Somebody got on.'

'A lady,' said she, nodding. 'Quite the beauty, so Diggory thought. Did you not chance to see her?'

'A glimpse only, and at night; I saw little. What was her name?'

Berengaria had to think on the question a moment, before it came to her mind. 'Ysabelon, methinks, or something like.'

'She's here, then.' Berengaria had never heard Tib Brackenbury speak with such reverence; she looked up in surprise. The man looked ready to genuflect before the throne, though it sat empty. Only then did it strike her how much he'd changed — how profound an alteration a spot of rain could bring.

'That's your queen?' she said, adding an orchid to her hair. 'That lady?'

'That lady, and Gower Bordekin, my king.'

'Two fey monarchs on our homely tree? How honoured we were.' She spoke sourly enough that even Brackenberry noticed, and looked at her strangely.

'Well, and where are they now?' added she, looking about, as though a Moon-Queen might pop out at any moment from a thicket somewhere, or a Sun-King from behind a tree.

'I don't know,' said Brackenberry. 'Why isn't she here?'

Berengaria, her interest waning, only shrugged.

'And,' added Brackenberry, another thought occurring to him. 'Where is Plumwood?'

A creak came, when his words died away: a faint, low sound, as of a bough swaying in the wind. No being of earthly good sense, like Berengaria, would have taken it for an answer; but Brackenberry had ceased to be such a creature, from the moment the first droplets of rain had touched his skin.

'Ho, there!' said Brackenberry at once, pacing the outskirts of the glade in search of the source. 'Did someone speak? Who's here?'

The creaking came again, and movement with it: something swayed into the glade, and paused on the edge of it, well away from the throne.

A tree.

A small one, this time, no rival whatsoever to the Kottow sort. Youthful, with smooth, supple bark, in a hue which, in stronger light, might prove to be goldish. Graceful branches shadowed the moss-carpet below, each flourishing with verdure.

To Berengaria's intrigued eye, the sapling had a headdress of sparkling mist, wreathed all among the slender boughs.

'What is this, now?' said she, when Brackenberry did not speak.

'A dryad of the glade,' answered he, gazing upon the sapling with rapt eyes. 'Not one of the queen's; she is too young.' He bowed to the golden tree, or the dryad, as he spoke, and unless Berengaria's fancy made away with her sense, the tree's elegant branches dipped in response.

And then came a glimpse of something among the verdure there, or more rightly, *someone,* for that was a loose tangle of hair draped over the youthful boughs, and a face: brown as a nut, and childlike.

'What's your name, child?' said Brackenberry, gently. 'And what will you with us?'

'I am Mabet,' she whispered. 'Thrice-removed great-child of the Grand Dame, and I've a message for thee.'

Brackenberry considered this eminence enough to warrant a low bow. 'An honour, Mabet of the Grand Dame's line. What's the message?'

'Who's the Grand Dame?' whispered Berengaria, a question which, for the present, Brackenberry waved away.

'It's this,' said Mabet softly. She composed her little face, and began to speak, in a more sing-song fashion, as though reciting from memory: 'If thou wouldst recover the Midsummer Queen, look thou into Winter, for there was trickery done.'

'Old Mother Winter,' said Brackenberry, grimly. 'I might have known she'd have something to do with it.'

'*Who,* if you please, is Old Mother Winter?' said Berengaria, with a trace of impatience. 'Or the Grand

Dame, either.'

'There is a queen of Winter, too,' said Brackenberry quickly. 'She is older than the Summer, far older, and — cold. She has had her jealous eyes on the Summertide this many an age, and found a way to wrest the forest from their Majesties, it seems.'

'Not the whole forest,' whispered Mabet. 'But a great part lies under ice, and another burns under a pitiless sun. 'Tis the Grand Dame's message to thee, passed down in all the days of her absence, 'til it should be wanted.'

'*She* has been absent, has she?' cried Brackenberry, his quick mind rapidly at work; and then he laughed. He laughed so hard he fell down, and sat in the earth, all the fern-leaves about him quivering with his mirth. Berengaria did not think he was amused, exactly; the laughter came from some other place, or some other feeling. 'Ah, and Grand she is, indeed!' he sighed at last, when he had composed himself. He got to his feet, and grinned at Berengaria. ''Twas the eldest of the Dryad-Trees as brought us home,' he said. 'The Grand Dame, this little one's great-mother, thrice removed. She's as old as the forest itself, if not older.'

'The Kottow Tree?' said Berengaria, aghast. 'She's a *Dryad*?'

'A Dryad-tree,' corrected Brackenberry. 'And what else could it be, after all? No one has yet managed to keep a Dryad-Tree out of somewhere she had a mind to venture into.' He smiled at Mabet, more gently, and added: 'She's home, child, if you've a mind to see her, though I don't know precisely where in the Forest she is just now.'

The little flower-face lit up; Mabet said: 'And 'twas said she went after the King; is that so?'

'Aye, and found him as well. Found every one of us, though it took her a hundred years; and now here we are, with a fine mess to mend.' He stood with his hands on his hips, thinking. 'It's perhaps too much to hope that we're to find the lot of them still with the Tree. No doubt they're scattered over the forest by now, much as we are. But it's a start. Mabet, think you that you could find your Grand Dame, if you tried?'

'If not I, then my sisters, of a certainty,' said Mabet. 'Shalt thou come up? We'll go at once.'

'And Berengaria, too?' said Brackenberry.

Mabet eyed the girl with some doubt. 'She is not of the forest. I think me she is a mortal.'

'Aye, but a fair and a fine one at that. I've need of her.'

'*Have* you, Tib Brackenbury?' said Berengaria, with a doubt to match Mabet's. 'Why?'

He made a face at that, but passed over her use of his mortal name. ''Tis the Grand Dame's judgement I trust,' he said. 'Most of us she's brought were Forest-folk to begin with, save only one or two. She's collected you for a reason.'

This made Berengaria's face sour again, though she couldn't have said why. Only a strange, and unsettling feeling of being far out of her depth, and uncertain of her place in this magical wood. But she made no further protest, for she wouldn't have had Brackenberry wander off with Mabet the Dryad, and leave her behind.

Up she went, then, into the sapling's wiry boughs, along with Brackenberry. And away they wandered, out of the queen's bower and back into the depths of the forest.

YSABELON

It was of no wonder at all, Ysabelon thought, that Peronel's temper should be so sour, or that the thaumaturge, Mermadak, should have chosen to sleep away a century. They were Summertide folk, every one of them, lost in the depths of Winter due to *her* foolish mistake. To be tricked by Mother Winter! Not once, but *twice*. For a time after her Remembering, so consumed with rage was she as to be incapable of clear thought. She knew only a wordless fury, a deep desire to rend *something* to pieces — the Winter Queen, by preference — until the balance should be restored, and the Summertide all her own again.

When these pleasant reflections had passed, Ysabelon found her sense and her feet both, and drew herself up as tall as she could.

'Where,' said she, with dangerous softness, 'is Mother Winter?'

'Who's to say?' answered Peronel. 'Not here. Elsewhere in the forest, no doubt.'

'I must find her,' said Ysabelon, Moon-Queen, and if the visions the prospect roused amidst the many elegances of her mind had little of compassion about them, well, who was to blame for that, save Winter herself? Had *she* not taken the Summer out of the Moon-Queen's heart, and darkened it? She had made for herself an implacable foe.

Peronel misliked the smile adorning her lady-liege's face, for she took a slight step back. 'How are you to do that, when the Court is closed? You'll not reach the greater forest, Majesty.'

'Shall I not? Who is to stop me? My Court cannot *like* to be snow-bound.'

But she paused, where she might have marched away at once, for a great many thoughts jostled for attention in her head, and she had not yet made sense of them all.

It had not taken her long to understand the identity of Gower Bordekin, nor to realise how many other folk of the Tree had their roots in this lost forest. 'Mend these folk, thaumaturge, if you please,' she said absently, as these ideas entered her mind. 'They are my brother's people, and do not deserve such a fate.' Her pointing finger indicated the two fey-shaped ice sculptures, forlorn little figures marooned not far from Mermadak's own tree.

And as Mermadak thawed out the two statues — receiving a ringing blow from an ice-crusted ladle, for his pains — Ysabelon mused some more.

Her brother. She and he had been so near to one

another; quartered up and down the trunk of the same Dryad-Tree — and if only their paths had crossed a little sooner!

No matter. A day or two only might have been saved, if they had. She must find him again; sooner, mayhap, than she sought the Winter Queen. Mother Winter might be wily, and full of tricks, but an oath was an oath, and a deal a deal. All Lady Frost need do was clasp hands with the Sun's King once more, and all would be mended.

Then she might wreak whatever revenge she chose, and with her brother's help to do it.

The notion pleased her; she smiled.

Only, what might have become of Gowerlon, out in the forest somewhere? Would she find him, tamely seated halfway up the Kottow Tree (as was), awaiting her return?

No. He would be gone somewhere, and to find *him* might be as great a challenge as to find Mother Winter herself.

'I do not quite know how to proceed,' she admitted at last, wishful of advice. 'Peronel. Mermadak. What think you? My brother is returned along with me, but I have not seen him. Nor shall I yet, methinks.'

'That'd be Gower,' nodded the creature with the ladle, a dumpy thing with a cobweb skirt and an expression of extreme displeasure. 'And if I've said once there was sommat *odd* about him, I've said it a hundred times.'

'Not a word have you said upon any such subject,' protested her companion, a sprightly-looking young fellow with an especially fine set of boots on him.

'Have, as well.'

'Have not. Why, you'd forgotten your own name, *Mudling,* like the rest of us.'

'I had remembered it, near enough. So did you, Willow-Wild.'

Ysabelon intervened. 'Could either of you find him? You are *his* Courtiers, are not you?'

'Aye,' said the one called Mudling. 'But what of that? We go when summoned; elsewise, we have not the least notion of his whereabouts.'

'We could go back to the Tree,' put in Willow-Wild. 'Mayhap he's there.'

'And where is that, now? The Tree tends to wander.'

Willow-Wild shrugged his thin shoulders.

Mudling folded her arms, her ladle swinging. 'Well, and how long are we to stand here arguing about what's best to do, and doing nothing at all?'

'A fair rebuke, Mudling,' said Ysabelon.

'This Tree you speak of,' interposed Peronel. 'Is that Merigot's?'

'I imagine it is,' answered Ysabelon. 'And Merigot is with it, if I'm not mistaken.'

'Oh?' said Mudling. 'Who's that?'

'*We* knew her as Mother Gantry.'

Peronel gave a crow of delight, uncharacteristically for her. Joy lit up the planes of her face, long frozen with cold and dissatisfaction; for a moment, Ysabelon saw her own Courtier again, a lady of Summertide, warmth and light, and good cheer.

The effect did not long last, but it would be brought forth soon again. Ysabelon swore it.

'You would like to see her, would you?' said she to Peronel.

Her Maid of Honour only nodded, but a faint

184

glow remained in her eyes: a glow of anticipation.

'Well, thaumaturge,' said Ysabelon, turning to Mermadak, who had absented himself from this flow of conversation, being engaged in an attempt at cleaning a smear of congealed soup from his hose. 'What skills have you to offer us?'

Mermadak looked up, frowning. 'I'm to have the honour of untangling this thicket of troubles, am I? Obliged to you.'

'You've magic about you.'

'As do you, Majesty, if you've forgotten.'

So she had. Those long, serene hours spent feasting under the moon's soft glow came to her mind; and bathing in the cooling flow of the rain, and all the deep magic it brought with it.

Did she need the clasp of her brother's hand, to set all to rights? The forest had not forgotten her; she felt that, down to her bones. It would welcome her return. And *one* concession she'd wrought from the tricksy Queen of Winter, at least: she was no longer forced to cart the snow about with her, and drown the wood in rime, wherever she stepped. Why, that was almost as good as being her own self again!

'Peronel, and Mermadak,' said she, 'Mudling and Willow-Wild. You'll all attend me, I trust, for I have need of you.'

'And where are we going?' said Mudling.

'We are going to talk to the rain.'

'*Talk* to the rain?' scoffed Mudling, though she trotted along in the pacing Ysabelon's wake gamely enough. 'And what are you going to say to it, pray?'

'I shall entreat its aid,' answered her queen. 'Though it will be no easy thing to accomplish, and it cannot be done here. I must get out of the Winter.'

And she wandered off, with the same blithe confidence as the Kottow Tree; trusting that her roots would take her wherever she wanted to go.

'What a pity the Dryad-Trees are all asleep in the Winter,' said she as she walked, an aside addressed mainly to Peronel and Mermadak. 'They might have walked you away from here the sooner.'

'They wouldn't wake,' said Peronel, with a scornful glance at the thaumaturge: presumably his efforts at rectifying this inconvenience had not impressed Peronel. 'Nor shall they now, I'll wager.'

'Not until the Summertide's restored,' Ysabelon agreed. 'But it won't be long now.'

'And *you* mean just to stroll out of the Court, do you?' said Peronel. 'Like as though you were a Dryad-Tree your own self.'

'She has the feet for it,' said Mudling unexpectedly.

'And the eyes to see her way,' put in Willow-Wild, nodding. 'If you've those two things, all you need do after that is *know*.'

'I didn't *know*, until you did,' said Mudling, incomprehensibly.

'Nor did I, 'till you did.'

Mudling smacked him with the ladle.

'Know *what?*' interposed Peronel.

'Where you're going,' said Willow-Wild, in some surprise.

'That isn't precisely it,' said Ysabelon. 'You can go a long way, you know, without having the first idea of where it is you are going *to*. The trick is to keep putting one foot in front of the other.'

'So says the Moon-Queen,' muttered Peronel, rebellious. 'The snow wouldn't let *us* saunter out, whatever we did with our feet.'

'Keeping wanderers *in* has been more its purpose than keeping them out,' Ysabelon concurred, with a fleeting glance at Mudling and Willow-Wild. 'But now we are going out,' and these words she spoke in a higher, stronger voice, pitching her words to reach the winds and the skies. 'I am the Winter Queen, and I will not be gainsaid!'

Nor was she. A blizzard, springing up swift and sudden, may have done its best to dissuade her, with the help of a freezing gale, but Ysabelon's steps did not falter. When the ice-bound winds reached a shrieking pitch, and bid fair to toss her into a snow-drift, Ysabelon merely raised her voice still further.

'*ENOUGH!*'

The word tossed and howled and screamed through the Winter Court, setting the skies a-shake. When the last echoes of it died away, they took the wind away with it, and the snow-storm too.

Into the sudden silence came the sound of Mudling coughing.

'Are you well?' said Willow-Wild, suspiciously.

Mudling spat out a mouthful of glittering snowflakes, and nodded.

'I would dearly like to know the *how* of that,' said Mermadak, at Ysabelon's elbow.

'I will teach you, on some other day,' said Ysabelon, scanning what she could see of the horizon with keen, sharp eyes. 'Not now. There: do I deceive myself, or are we bidding fair for an exit?'

The forest-hall that was her Court still proposed to go on forever, or near it, but somewhere behind the parade of stationary Trees and rich furniture there came a fleeting glimpse of emerald-green.

'I see it,' said the thaumaturge, narrowing his eyes.

'I, also,' agreed Peronel, adding tartly, 'It shall not take us much above a week to reach it, I suppose.'

'Not more than five minutes,' said Mudling stoutly, and she was right, for as the five of them advanced upon the distant flicker of hope, walking with a settled purpose, that desired horizon drew rapidly nearer. Soon it seemed to hover just beyond the next stand of Trees; and then, just a step away.

Ysabelon's first footfall into that soft carpet of green brought a stray tear to her eyes. Ahh, the Summer... there it lay, drowsing this long while, but so close now to a wakening. She could feel it, smell the latent verdure upon the air, sense the deep magic of it, *so close,* just behind a thin veil...

Peronel seemed still more profoundly affected. She sank both feet deep into the greenery, and stood with her eyes closed, her fingers gripping Mermadak's shoulder so hard as to draw a grimace to his face.

'I had forgotten,' said she, softly, taking vast, deep breaths. 'The *scent* of it, the...'

Words failed her, which, as Ysabelon could now remember, was not at all characteristic of Peronel.

Even Mermadak was not unmoved. His customary expression of sardonic detachment did not alter, but his throat worked, and an odd sheen glimmered in his eyes.

'Well,' said Ysabelon, briskly. 'There will be time for lingering later. For now, to work.'

She paused then, turned her focus away from the fresh spring woodland all around her (for the gusting cold of the Winter Court at her back had soon melted away, leaving a soft breeze instead).

'I wonder if I might still...' she murmured, and then grinned, and crowed aloud as her feet left the ground. Her wings! Shimmer they might with ice-light now, sending wafts of frost-flurry into the wind, but they bore her still, and up she rose.

'Come, Mermadak!' she called. 'Come, Peronel! To the high places we go!'

She did not think of Mudling, or Willow-Wild; why would she? They were her brother's folk, no Courtiers of hers, and they were back in the greater forest now. She did not think of them again until much later, when the work was done, and some stray remembrance brought them to mind.

For the present, she had need only of Peronel and Mermadak, if of anyone at all. *They* had the will and the magic to keep pace with her, Peronel borne aloft by a gauzy set of wings not unlike her own, and Mermadak swept upwards by a wisp of something cloud-like and swift. They did not know where she proposed to go, and nor did she. But she *knew*, once more, that some sense would lead her aright; some latent fancy, some flicker of magic, would carry her along.

Up and up she went, until she broke through the enveloping canopy of the trees. And then the flight tugged deeply at her memory, for was this not among the last of the things she had done, before she'd met Old Mother Winter? The memory of *that* ill-fated flight was strong in her mind as she drifted over the half-drowsing forest, and for a moment she wished, with a fierce will, that some other fancy had caught at her on that fateful night. Had she but been contented to feast, and sing, and play at mummeries with her Court! A hundred years of *wrongness* might then have been averted.

But it is useless to dwell over the past, and curse

the former self for its blunders. Ysabelon, too practical a woman, and too very much a queen, to linger long in such reflections, soon gave up the idea. Whatever had gone awry in the past, she had the power, now, to mend it; and mend it she would, but not with weeping.

There. There, rising aloft, high above the old, lost forest: there was a swirl of deeper mist, a thick fog of clouds, and a tapestry of boughs peeping through it. Ysabelon turned her face that way, smiling.

'The ancients?' protested Peronel, her gaze following her queen's. 'Surely you do not propose to talk to *them*?'

'Who else is to persuade the rain?' answered Ysabelon serenely.

'But— but they are *cruel.*'

'They are no such thing. If some among those who've ventured into the Grove have come out again in an odd state, it is due to no malice of the ancients.'

'To what, then, *is* it due?' snapped Peronel, but this Ysabelon did not choose to answer, having no special wisdom to offer, mayhap, or no attention to spare for the matter just then.

'Try not to breathe in too much of the fog,' she recommended, as she drifted down, down, into the mist-wreathed Grove where the eldest of the Dryad-Trees slumbered.

If those arbours out in the greater forest were vast, there are not the words to express the proportions of the ancients. Too elderly now, and too sere, to wander, as their younger selves had done, and their descendants did still, these Trees — and their Dryad-Companions — slept fitfully atop a great swell of ground overlooking the forest. So high did their knotted branches reach, they mingled with the clouds; and, indeed, that was what brought them to the high places of the forest. Up there, the mists they wore threaded through their own hair might blend with the skies, merging the deep, emerald magic of their ancient roots with the wild magic of the heavens.

The rain, some said, was the result.

Ysabelon came down gently there, her toes sinking into a fragrant morass of earth and leaf, moss and blossom, dust and dew. The air smelled fresh and sharp, as though a thunderstorm had but just passed through. There was not too much mist down here among the jutting roots, though velvet moss grew thickly up the craggy trunks, and the soft breezes of a butterfly's flight stirred the air about her ears.

Ysabelon laid a hand against one such trunk, gently ushering away a cluster of bright-winged, feasting butterflies. She looked up, and up, into the arching branches far above her.

'Thaumaturge,' said she, trusting that Mermadak heard her.

'My queen,' came his voice, from somewhere nearby.

'Make a tree of me.'

He spluttered something incomprehensible; so did Peronel.

'A tree? A *tree!* My queen — Lady Frost, so preposterous an idea—'

'It is no such thing,' said Ysabelon. 'I cannot reach the ancients as I am, and their Dryads are too deep in slumber to hear my voice from here. What, then, am I to do? How does one talk to a Tree, Mermadak?'

The silence was heavy with his gropings for an answer.

'Precisely,' she said. 'But there can be no difficulty in holding converse with a Tree if one is leafy one's own self. Unless Peronel has some other notion?'

Peronel did not, though this did not prevent her from echoing Mermadak's disapproval. 'We have but *just* had you come back to us,' said she, glowering. 'Are you now to be lost as a Tree, for another hundred years?'

'I trust not. I shall have the two of you here to turn me back.'

Peronel snorted.

Mermadak gave an irritable sigh. 'Your faith in my thaumaturgical arts is heart-warming.'

Ysabelon turned her head to grin at him. 'As I've said before,' she said, 'if you *know* you are able to do it, then you shall.'

His scowl deepened. 'I don't *know* that at all.'

'But I do, and I shall lend you my confidence.'

'Her Majesty is gracious.' Sourly spoken.

'Am I not?' Her smile widened.

He grumbled something else, but wasted no further time on remonstrance. 'Very well, but if it goes wrong I hope you know we shall blame you *entirely*—'

The rest of his sentence was lost to her, for in the midst of his grumblings he had done something clever and enchanting; Ysabelon felt the effects of it through to her bones. Predominantly in the fact that, *afterwards*, she no longer possessed any. Nor had she hair, or eyes, or feet; in their places she had a heavy tangle of roots, thrusting deep, deep down into the earth. She towered over her two Courtiers; though in height she could never hope to rival the ancients about her, she had far surpassed that of a mere fey.

A brisk wind ruffled her branches, tossing her leaves into a cheerful rustle. The sensation so entranced her that she forgot herself, for an unknowable time.

She was roused by whispering, a different sort to any she had heard before. The susurration of wind-swept leaves was no unfamiliar thing to what had once been her ears, but never before had she understood anything like *words* winding through it.

'C-cold…' whispered the leaves. '*Whence comes the cold?*'

This surprised Ysabelon, for the earth and air felt warm enough to her.

But somewhere below, in the deep earth, she detected a hint of something else: a note of creeping cold, emanating from that Winter-bound part of the forest. Her own, lost Court.

Were she greater, grander and older, like the ancients around her, how far would her roots go? Right into the Winter, no doubt.

'*C-cold,*' whispered the ancients again, deep in slumber, and dreaming. '*Why the cold?*'

'Actually,' said Ysabelon, with a shuffle of her own leaves. 'That is what I am here to talk about.'

No easy task, to penetrate the deep fog of their dreaming, and insert her own ideas and needs into their thinkings. They were befuddled, having left waking and clear thought behind them long ago. She could not wake them, nor could she reason with them; they were naught but a whorl of impressions, of drifting notions all tumbled together, and with the penetrating cold lancing through it all.

So she wove them a dream, instead. These ancient minds, lost so long in a fog of their own dreaming, they soaked up the Moon-Queen's visions like rainwater. She showed them her snow-drowned Court, where the rain froze before it touched the ground, turned as brittle and hard as Old Mother Winter's heart. And she gave them another seeing: a warming of the land under the snow, a gentling of the firmament above, where the storm-clouds massed themselves for another deluge of ice. Through her, they saw the rain fall at last, a mighty monsoon of warm, Summer rain; and the ice turned to silver river-water, and flowed away, and beneath the perishing blanket of snowfall there were moon-flowers, her favourites, beginning to unfurl.

In her mind's eye, and theirs, she saw the Winter wash away in a flourish of colour, and the Summertide put back, just the way she had left it.

Not so far away, in what had *been* the Winter Court these hundred years gone, a quantity of spiritless Courtiers looked up at the welkin whorls above, and mutters of confusion and annoyance went up: at the splashes of darker colour marring the beauty of a silken gown; at the ruin of a pastry or a tart, soggy with rain; at the flow of good wine over the floor, a silver goblet fallen prey to a startled movement, a sudden departure.

The rain would spare nothing; Lady Moonlight had willed it so. The lords and ladies of her Court, resplendent in their sodden silks and dripping hair, watched the tempest sweep the vestiges of their torment away; and only then, when the frozen Dryad-Trees woke with a shake of their hair, and took a turn about the hall; when the flowers put forth their Summer raiment, and poured perfume into the air; when fine silverware turned back into sticks and branches and velvet-clad divans into mossy-carpeted stones; *then* did they understand.

So it was that the devotees of *one* Court, at least, danced again: a rain-soaked galliard, feet and voices lifted high in celebration. And the Dryads swept the sleep from their eyes, crept down from their lofty couches, and joined in.

Ysabelon had not quite the eyes to see so far as that, but she *felt* some of it, and rejoiced in every returning glow of warmth that reached her roots, and washed over her leaves.

As did the ancients surrounding her. No more aware of the events at her Court than they were of Ysabelon's presence, they nonetheless felt the ebbing of the cold; and, eased, slipped into a quieter slumber.

'Well,' rustled Ysabelon, a syllable of profound satisfaction, and she spent a moment there, standing tall with her borrowed branches raised high, smiling in her treeish way at a good day's work well done.

Then: 'And now, what? I am a tree, and I must be a woman again.'

Though, were she to own it, she was not free from sorrow at the prospect, for there was peace in the being of a tree; the sleepy, gentle patience of a slow-growing thing, nothing like the bustle of the ephemeral world of Kottow (or of Lambelin, Oakham and Ryle); nor like the merry frivolity of her Court, either. To let her roots delve deeper into the earth, settle her there, and watch the centuries pass in peace and silence: *there* was beauty.

And with these thoughts surfacing in the slowing processes of her mind, Ysabelon knew she had got by far too much mist tangled up in her hair, had let the soft fog slip too far into her dreams.

'Mermadak,' she said, turning about, in hope of finding him there. 'Thaumaturge? Peronel! I am ready, and should dearly love to be a woman again, and fey, however hurly-burly a life it shall be — Mermadak? Peronel!'

She did not see them, nor feel them anywhere about her, and she wondered.

But she felt *something*: a touch upon the roots of herself, where the tops of them protruded from the earth. Many soft touches there, like the scurrying of tiny feet — it *was* the scurrying of tiny feet, a great crowd of soft-furred creatures having set their paws all over her. They were swarming up her trunk, and dancing in the branches of her hair: red-jacketed, black as her beloved night, or white as the reviled snows of her twisted Court: so many of them.

They seemed happy about something.

And in their wake, people came, though not the ones she sought. She saw Mauvian, the one they'd called Maut Fey, back at the Kottow Tree; Diggory Stokey, that gentle soul, stout and sturdy and sound as a tree himself; and Gower Bordekin, or Gowerlon, her disgraceful wanderer of a brother, with the sun wreathed all in his mane of hair, and two Courtiers trailing behind him.

They gathered at the base of her trunk, this motley lot, and stood staring up into her branches with a collective befuddlement so palpable she could almost have bathed in it.

'I think your squirrels have taken to madness, Maut,' said Gowerlon at last. 'Those frisks denote celebration, if I'm not mistaken, yet all they've found is a Tree.'

The fools ought not to linger here, where the mist

could get into their eyes; did they not *know* that, having wandered for a hundred years in a daydream? An irritable twitch of her boughs brought a swift rain of silver-skinned apples down onto their heads. Hah! She had not known herself to be an apple-tree. The thought pleased.

Something fruitish rode on her brother's shoulder, too: a furred thing, but plum-hued, and now it clambered down his long frame and joined its fellows in scampering about her roots.

Then it wandered off, but not far, for soon came a voice she knew, and had briefly lost: Mermadak's.

'*PLUMWOOD*?' bellowed he, voice and — there — footsteps coming nearer. 'What, does the shape amuse you, rogue? A squirrel! Peronel, *what* think you to that — a squirrel, if you please, and the whole Court a-search for him these several ages at least—'

Peronel's voice cut in: 'Compose yourself, thaumaturge, and make him fey-shaped again, for I think me he's stuck. And when you're finished with that, *here* is the Lady-Tree, stationary at last, and if you do not change her back quickly she's like to wander off again.'

'The Lady-Tree?' said Diggory Stokey, and glanced up at her with a smile. 'What, is it you, my lady Ysabelon?'

'Ah!' said Maut. 'Then the squirrels are not out of their wits; they've solved the mystery, whether we've the wit to know it or not.'

Gowerlon, her disgrace of a king, sat down upon her roots with a laugh, and raised a goblet of something pungent in her direction. Where he had conjured up such a thing seemed scarcely worth asking, save that she hoped he might muster another for her. 'Apples!' he called. 'Doubtless you'll be wanting a wine of them, before long. Peronel, take note.'

Peronel gave a sigh, but Ysabelon thought it more a rehearsed response than a genuine one, for the sun was shining in her face again, and the smile would not be repressed. She bent and gathered an armful of the silver-fresh fruit, even as poor Mermadak, harassed and irked, made a fey-thing out of the squirrel they called Plumwood, and proved his senses aright.

'*LORD!*' cried that liberated fellow, when he had lips and tongue again to speak; whether the word was a greeting or a profanity did not seem to trouble the Summer-King, who mayhap took it as both, and was no less pleased for it. Gowerlon stood up again, tossed his goblet away, and caught up the spindly-shanked Plumwood in a rough embrace.

Plumwood repeated this uncouth greeting with all those present, progressing to a startled Maut Fey, and her brother's Courtiers (Quince and Barleythorn, that was their names); not omitting a laughing Diggory Stokey, nor Peronel either.

Ysabelon's attention was fixed upon Mermadak the while, for he had seated himself at the base of her trunk, and sat there, breathing.

Peronel noticed. 'Well, thaumaturge? There's a lady still missing.'

Mermadak made an irritable gesture. 'Aye, I've not forgotten. This thaumaturgy lark is no simple thing, mind. I'm out of breath.'

Mist crept down out of the boughs, and wreathed in his hair; Ysabelon wafted it away. Fool of a thaumaturge, thought she: do not delay! The fog will not spare this merry band a second time, any more than it did the first; and though to be Ysabelon of Lambelin, or Oakham, or Ryle, had not displeased her, for the life had brought many consolations with it, she had no fancy to repeat the adventure.

But Mermadak got himself together, aided, no doubt, by the peremptory ministrations of Peronel. And then fell he to work, and Ysabelon forgot her treeish musings, and became a hurly-burly fey again.

And when restored to four limbs, and wings, and a fey-woman's soft rope of hair, she spoke up at once.

'Get you out of this grove! Have you *no* sense between you? The mist!' She turned up her face and her hands in protest, for the mist drifted down and down, and bid fair to swallow them all.

But Gowerlon, with a cheek of a smile, summoned up a breeze redolent of morning, and sent the fog streaming away. 'I am not entirely heedless,' claimed he, a statement productive of a snort from Peronel (and his sister, too).

Ysabelon held out her hand to him. 'Such trouble as you've caused, with your *long walk,* brother, I've a mind more to beat you than greet you. But Old Mother Winter promised, and if you'll clasp hands with me, there is much that will be set to rights.'

Gowerlon's response was a befuddled frown; he said: 'What's this? I've a bone to pick with *you*, sister, for what business had you to go following me? I'd have found my way back in time—'

'Psh,' interjected Peronel, 'only with Merigot's help at that—'

'—and *someone*,' went on Gowerlon, ignoring this, 'ought to have been watching over the forest.'

'I did an ancient a good turn,' said Ysabelon. 'A foolish turn as well, and I've paid for it. We all have.

Berate me later; I'll berate you as well, and a fine quarrel we shall have. But for the present, waste no more time: shake hands with me.'

The Summer-King, swallowing the words that rose to his lips in retort, did so; and it seemed to Ysabelon that, all about her, the forest exhaled: a long, soft, verdant sigh, scented with moss-damp.

'Well, then,' said the Moon-Queen, briskly. 'That's that.'

'Not quite,' said Gowerlon. 'I've a displaced crone to evict from my Court. Shall you aid me, sister?'

'In penance for my gullibility? Aye, that is fitting.'

'Come, then. The rest of you: Merigot will tend to you. I'd go there at once, were I you, for the mist has got into your eyes after all, and she'll clear it away.'

It was true, for Maut and Diggory, and Barleythorn and Quince (and even Plumwood, a little) had turned dreamy-eyed and vague; linger much longer, and they would be forgetting themselves again, and Dreaming up yet another life.

'Your Court, then, brother?' said Ysabelon, mustering her wings: they flourished in Summer-glow once more, the ice-light all gone.

Gowerlon's boots left the earth: he turned his face to the south. 'Methinks it will not take long,' said he, grimly, and flew away; and Ysabelon followed.

THE SUMMER LORD-AND-LADY

When the disturbers of Nature are removed, it loses no time in righting itself.

Gowerlon and his royal sister swept down out of the clear skies into the midst of the crone's Summer Court, and found it changing already. Gone was the withering heat, ebbing away like the tide; Gower felt it recede farther with every breath, every step that he took into his reclaimed kingdom. An intrepid duo of clouds, more eager or more reckless than their brethren, took it upon themselves to waft over the heat-blasted fields, and disgorge themselves of a neat flurry of cool, drenching rain; the parched grass soaked it up, emitting a grateful swell of clean, sweet scent.

Gower took this in with hearty inhalations, a smile

wreathing his face as the rain beaded in his hair. He looked about him at the wakening space, invigorated and refreshed (he and the land, both); and when he had breathed in his fill, and satisfied himself that all was on the way to mending, he lifted his face, and cried at a sky-shattering volume: '*LET THE FALSE QUEEN SHOW HERSELF.*'

'I wasn't a false queen,' came a calm voice at his elbow. 'I had your sister's blessing.'

'You had no such thing,' said Ysabelon, a wrathful vision, advancing upon Old Mother Winter with the storm-clouds gathering behind her eyes. 'I granted you an interval only, and how did you repay me for that kindness?'

'I took what I wanted,' said Mother Winter, a slight smile driving the wrinkles deeper into the harsh lines of her face. 'Would not you have done the same?'

'Never.' The word was spoken coldly, proudly.

'No?' Mother Winter, leaning heavily upon a knotted stick, wore a quantity of shawls thrown over her age-bowed shoulders, thick as a bank of snow-clouds. Her fathomless old eyes twinkled irrepressibly at the monarchs she had, temporarily, bested. 'Walk a span of ages in my old boots, milady, and you'll sing a different song.' She lifted one of the boots in question, to show it off: disreputable indeed, the thing, all the colour worn out of it, and the seams barely holding together.

Ysabelon's mind shied away from a knowledge of those span of ages; how long, *long* a while this ancient had reigned over the Winter, whether she would or no. She and Gowerlon, no children themselves, were but sprigs of spring in comparison.

Would not *she* grow weary of the settled chill, the paralysing cold? Never to feel the warm Summer rain again! Never to feel the silken moss under her toes, or the heartening warmth of her brother's sunglow on her upturned face. Would not she do anything at all to resign such a role?

Still.

'You cannot wonder at my anger,' said Ysabelon.

'Nor mine,' said Gower, grim as Winter himself.

'I do not wonder at it,' said Mother Winter. 'But I needn't be disturbed by it, either.' She grinned, and eased her old bones into a seated posture upon the sloping surface of a sun-warmed rock. The granite was bare, not a scrap of moss or leaf upon it: baked to barrenness by her merciless sun. 'I'll not go back,' said Mother Winter abruptly, and her smile vanished. 'Have your Summertide if you will; I'll not oppose you. But the Winter must get along without me.'

'The choice is not open to you,' said Gowerlon. 'Winter cannot be left untended. Left to itself, it would soon do far worse than you have, these hundred years!'

'Truth.' Mother Winter (as was) inclined her head. 'But that's no longer my concern.' The grin reappeared, an unlovely expression; truly, she seemed energised. 'I think I shall follow *your* example,' she added, and smiled up at Summer's siblings. 'I'll see what the world looks like, out past the borders of the forest.'

'But what of Winter?' Ysabelon demanded.

'What of it?'

'*Someone* must look after it.'

'Perhaps *someone* will,' said the crone. 'But it needn't be me.' She got up from her perch as she spoke, stretching out her shoulders, and it seemed to Gower's wondering eyes that already she moved easier. 'Now; where was it, the way Out?'

Neither answered her; she shrugged her bony shoulders, and tutted. 'Never mind. I'll find it.' Without bidding the Summer goodbye, she turned and wandered away, leaning still upon her knotted stick, but a little less now.

Gowerlon looked at his sister; she gazed back.

'What now?' said he.

'Do not look at me!' she said. 'I have had enough of Winter! It is your turn, brother.'

'I shan't go anywhere near Winter's Court.'

'That's wise, but then, who shall? None of my Court will have aught to do with it. A hundred years is enough for them, too.'

'If you imagine any of *my* Courtiers could be persuaded! What, to change all *this*—' and he stretched out his arms, spun in a circle, the gesture encompassing the whole clear-skied, fragrant, sun-warmed gloriousness of it all — 'for an ice-dunking, and a cold north wind? Faugh!'

'I will do it.'

The words came from someone new, whose approach had, in the urgency of the problem, gone unnoticed. Gowerlon looked round.

A Dryad-Tree stood some little distance away, a youngling, not tall yet, though stout enough to carry her Dryad *and* two others in her golden branches.

'Brackenberry?' said Gowerlon, frowning, but it was not he who had spoken.

'Aye,' said Brackenberry, beaming, and he jumped down at once to sweep his liege-lord the lowest of bows. 'Milord, and milady! What delight! I wish you both joy of your return, and all the land, too. And,' he turned back to the Dryad-Tree, and helped a young lady down from it, 'perhaps you remember the lady Berengaria?'

Gower did, though he had never had much speech with the girl. She looked... changed. The same fair hair, yes, and sky-coloured eyes, but that hair had got the wind bound up in it, and kept it there; and the eyes, as he watched, were already turning the crystal-hard, fathomless blue-white of new ice.

'Majesties,' smiled Berengaria, curtseying prettily. 'What think you? Shall you let me join your fellowship? I'll take this problem from your shoulders, and gladly.'

Gowerlon stared. 'Brackenberry,' he said after a moment, 'pray explain. What brings you here — and you, leafling—' (here he inclined his head, with great respect, to the little Dryad still up in the boughs) '— and why in all that's shining would anybody want the mantle of Winter?'

'We were looking for the Kottow Tree,' said Brackenberry. 'The Kottow Tree *as was*, that is, for I doubt me that Merigot, or Mother Gantry, calls it that still. We didn't find her. Come to think of it, Mabet, what did bring us here? If anyone of us would know, it's you.'

The leafling, shy in the presence of Summer's lady and lord, spoke up but softly. 'I went where my roots took me,' she said. 'I thought that would be Mother Merigot, and her Tree.'

'Ah!' cried Brackenberry merrily. 'But we're here instead, and in time to hear somewhat of your dilemma. Well, Berengaria? What have you to say of Winter?'

'I've no fear of an ice-dunking,' said she, a curious little smile playing about her mouth. 'Or a cold north wind, either. I would make a fine queen, me: I've always known it. And in *my* Winter, there'll be a deep chill, to be sure; a fine, bone-deep freeze to strip the flesh from the bones. And there will be vicious gales, when I should chance to be in a poor mood, bringing a blizzard with them; and all the waters frozen over.' These prospects, bleak to the imagination of most, seemed to please Berengaria; Gowerlon shivered a little, somewhere within.

Berengaria continued: 'And since they are, we'll skate upon them, with silver blades strapped to our feet. And when the gales are howling about the land we'll take to the Court, where the great fires are built, and drink warmed wine with spices. We shall feast upon meat and pastries—'

'Almond tarts,' put in Ysabelon. 'And marchpane.'

'Yes! And there'll be silks enough to keep out the cold, and tapestries. And all the beauty there is in the cool shimmer of ice, and the glitter of snow, I'll deck the Winter in it all, and the Court, too. And then, you know, it shall not be so very bad, at all.'

She was smiling as she spoke, her eyes ice-bright, and Gowerlon believed (though he hardly knew how) that she meant every word.

Brackenberry beamed upon them all, and clapped his hands. 'There! Our Merigot knew her business, and Mabet, too; a fine solution, is it not?'

Ysabelon stared at the girl, her face a picture of disbelief. 'Can you be sincere?' she said. 'Think, Berengaria! There'll be no getting out of it again, later.'

'Leastwise,' put in Gowerlon, 'not for a span of

ages, or more.'

'I am certain,' said Berengaria. 'Though I daresay I should like to pay a visit to the Summer, once in a while.'

'That can be permitted,' said Ysabelon, cautiously.

'And you may like to wander into the Winter, on occasion,' said Berengaria. 'You and all your Court! I shall ready the best of the marchpane for you, and the wine as well.'

Ysabelon, the fleeting taste of almond-tarts upon her tongue, did not demur.

Neither did Gowerlon.

'Then it's decided,' said Brackenberry, with a frisk of joy, as though he had arranged the matter himself. 'And all is well in the forest again: huzzah!'

So it was. Gowerlon felt the rightness of everything, like a discordant tune wrenched back into melody. He laughed, caught up the Moon-Queen in an embrace, and danced the pavane with her. She, losing what remained of her anger in an instant, went along with it, though she permitted herself a swat at his hair.

'Do not beat me,' he pleaded. 'You can see I am contrite.'

Far too merry was he for contrition; Ysabelon laughed. 'I know better than to expect such, from you,' she said. 'Promise me you'll not go *walking* again, brother.'

'I cannot promise forever,' said he. 'But not soon, Lady Moon. Not soon.'

MOTHER MERIGOT

Mother Gantry's part in this motley business was
finished the moment the Kottow Tree (her own Tree,
whether she knew it or no) had gathered up its roots
and leapt, all in a rush, back into the heart of the lost
forest. Then the work was done, the wanderers
returned, and she and her Tree both might consider
themselves freed from all further obligation. Or,
nearly. There was the mist to sweep from behind the
eyes of Barleythorn and Quince, of Plumwood and
Diggory and Maut (again). They submitted to a
scolding patiently enough, a remonstrance she felt
bound to give; for had the rain not *just* washed all the
dreaming off them?

And herself as well, she was bound to admit, for
the saucepan had not kept it out of her hair for very

long. And therein lay the source of the only anger she had known in many a year: that there had been aught about her for the rain to wash away. What could her own, dear Tree mean by it? *She* was not to be swaddled up in the fog of dreaming, set to the telling of a new tale, a new character entire. How *could* her Tree use her so? She was Merigot, of the tallest Tree in the forest; she was among the very oldest of those yet awake, near an ancient herself.

Thus had she gone about for some little time, tight-lipped and radiating displeasure. Though were she truthful about the source of it, it was not only the having been a sleepwalker, a waking dreamer, that angered her.

Were she honest, she had *liked* Mother Gantry. Given her choice of any role to play out in the wider world, she might have chosen just such a woman. Mother Gantry had good, sound sense, and a sturdiness about her belying the weathered map of wrinkles that she was. Her white hair had commanded the respect she deserved, and she'd been useful. The folk of the Tree, they had loved her, and she them.

'Twas these reflections which brought her back, at last, into a better humour. She had not suffered, she (except in her pride); and after all, mayhap her dear, wicked Tree had been right. What use had a plain market town for a Dryad — or a Dryad for Kottow?

And the work had been done, despite her dreaming. The Tree had gone patiently on, year after year, gathering in the forest-folk one by one, until at last the time for home-coming came. And she, Mother Gantry, had been there as she ought, tending to every bough, every leaf, almost as tenderly as she might have done as Merigot.

209

All, then, had turned out well.

All, indeed! For she'd felt the change in the air, when the Summertide came back in; the moment all was set, at last, to rights, even Mother Gantry knew it. Merigot, now: the Dryad in her let out a great, soft breath of relief, releasing a tension held so long she'd forgotten how to see it.

Everything was right again, then, save one only: Diggory Stokey.

Those who thought the good man slow of wit were far from the mark. She'd always thought so. Maybe he wasn't a deep-thinker, like some, but he saw far, and he saw quickly.

He'd seen the forest creep back into Mother Gantry's heart, seen the mists clear from the deep places of her eyes; seen, in fact, the moment when the dreaming faded away, and Merigot returned. All this he'd seen, before *she* had even puzzled it out herself.

But then, he had naught to distract him, like the others. Not for *him* a sweeping away of one life, and a return to another. The rain scarcely touched him, in fact, for there it had nothing to do. Diggory Stokey was not forest-folk. Like Berengaria Dow (for whom the forest held a special fate, as it has turned out), Diggory Stokey was mortal; not brought *back* to the forest, but simply brought, like an extra parcel caught up with the others. Or so he felt. And since this lost, mist-dreaming forest held no particular fate in store for him (unlike Berengaria), there he remained at the end of the mad midsummer tale: mortal still, a plain, simple soul lost in enchantment.

He sat by himself, as the forest-folk came in from their wanderings in the high places, and begged Mother Merigot for her aid. Cloaked in a deep silence most unlike him, he watched without speaking as they came in, laughing, and went out again the same; even Maut, Mauvian now, who he'd so long known (in his small, mortal way, at least — a mere handful of years compared to the many she'd wandered through); even Maut had barely seemed to remember him, wrapped up as she was in her new, or ancient, character, her squirrels and her friends, her feyness (no longer resented) and her enchantments.

The small creatures did not cluster about Diggory's knee, for he did not possess any wildness they recognised. The rain did not bathe him in magic, as it did the others; it held no magic that a plain man could use. He was not to go flying with Barleythorn and Quince, nor feasting with the fey-queen in her twilit bower.

Mayhap this last wounded him the most, for the lady Ysabelon had made no small impression on Diggory's honest heart. All the loyal devotion he possessed in his sound, steady soul, he'd been ready to lay at her feet; had done so already, without conscious thought, and he could not now take it back.

'Diggory,' said Mother Gantry (or Merigot; even she could not soon decide which name she presently preferred). 'Art thou well?'

He sat in her kitchen, tucked up on a carved stool he'd once made with his own, clever hands, wrapped still in his mantle of silence. He had no answer to give her, but she read one in the stricken look of his eyes: no, he was not well at all.

Her little kitchen was otherwise quiet, now, the fleet-footed wanderers having been and gone away again, back out into the woods and the rain. Mother Gantry fetched a pot of tea to offer, set a fragrant cup into his hands. He took it absently, sipped; something of the lost look faded from his eyes, just a little, and they sharpened.

'You are changed, Mother,' said he.

'I am, I think.' She looked down at herself, saw the same loved, but unlovely garments she'd worn these hundred years gone; the same wiry old limbs beneath, a little age-bowed, but not much. 'But then, much in me is the same.'

Diggory shook his head, stubborn man. 'We used to joke Maut, didn't we? Maut Fey we said, finding her with another squirrel tucked in the crook of her arm, or a wood-mouse hidden in her sleeve. She didn't like it *then*, but *now* she's...' His words trailed away, a frown digging deep folds in the broad expanse of his brow. 'She's fey right through to her heart, not a scrap of woman about her. They all are. Mudleaf and Willow Wildboots, Tib Brackenbury. Even *you*, our good Mother Gantry.'

'Aye,' she said. 'Does it trouble you so very much, Diggory?'

'And the lady,' he went on. 'A *queen*, and Gower Bordekin— I always thought him a bit odd, Mother, I fancy we all did, but a king has the right to be as odd as he chooses, no?'

These reflections growing jumbled, Mother Gantry could not follow, quite, the direction of Diggory's thoughts, save that he endured a degree of misery she did not precisely understand. He stopped speaking, his thoughts drifting off into silence, carrying him far from the simple comforts of her kitchen; his breath escaped in a sigh.

'Diggory Stokey,' she said sharply. 'Attend.'

His eyes refocused on her face, puzzlement

replacing the woe. 'Yes, Mother?'

'Think on this. *Why* does it trouble thee so? What matter if Maut *is* a wood-fey, and me a Dryad? What difference does Tib Brackenbury's nature make to *thee?*'

He thought, that good Diggory Stokey. It took him some time, and she saw the effort of it: a man not given to soul-searching had no easy road through such a task. But an answer came. 'Mayhap it's not their nature but mine,' he said slowly. 'I've been set apart, Mother, and I never used to be.'

'And?' she encouraged.

He went on. 'The folk of the Kottow-Tree; that's what we were. They were *my* people. That was my place; I was one of them, just the same. We were a band of misfits, weren't we? Odd folk, living up and down the strange, over-tall Tree on the edge of the town. They might have looked askance at us, Mother, but they accepted us, well enough: and we were happy.'

'They are not lost to thee. Nor am I.'

The trouble was not so easily to be beaten out of him as all that. 'Are they not?' he persisted. 'They're all gone, Mother; there's only you and me left, and soon you'll go back to your own folk among the Dryad-Trees and... Mother, where am *I* to go now? What's there for me here, or back in Kottow, either?'

Mother Gantry's fingers twitched; the handle of her trusty saucepan was so easily within reach, and a sound blow upon the head with it might do the man a world of good. She restrained the impulse, however, and refilled his cup. 'Drink that,' she commanded. 'And listen, Diggory Stokey. If you think those who've loved thee will forget thee in a trice, thou art doing them an injury. Wouldst *thou* so soon forget *them*? Wouldst thou forsake all you've loved, in pursuit of some new, shining thing?'

'Never.'

'Nor shall they. Mark thou my words. Our good Maut is a mite distracted at present, that's so. But if she isn't back here in her own house by the dawn, I shall — why, I shall throw away my saucepan! And it is a prime favourite with me, as all know.'

Diggory's eyes widened. 'Not the saucepan, Mother! Wager something else.'

'The saucepan,' repeated she, firmly. 'There isn't the smallest risk of its loss. Maut will be back, Diggory, and Tib as well. Mudleaf and Willow. Even Gower Bordekin, and Berengaria, and the lady. Not today, mayhap, nor tomorrow, for they've work to do. But they'll come. Them as finds a true home don't lightly throw it away again.'

He said nothing, yet, neither protest nor agreement. But the smile was creeping back into his eyes, and the weight of his trouble seemed to have left him, leaving him lightened; he sat taller.

'Now, help me a while,' she said, brisk again, and downed the remains of her tea. 'My poor, dear Tree cannot be praised enough for her efforts, but my *goodness*, has she made a mess! There's my house, and thine, to set to rights, and then we'd best take a look-in at Maut's and Tib's as well.'

'Right.' Diggory set down his cup, and rose. The Dryad was taken unawares by the swift, tight pressure of his embrace; he squeezed her thoroughly, and set her carefully down. 'You're a treasure, Mother Merigot. You, and your wayward Tree.'

'We know it.' She gave him her mischievous smile,

the twinkling one she'd often used in her distant youth. 'Broom's there in the corner,' she said.

Diggory, dutifully, took it up.

And she was right, the Dryad, of course. The night passed in velvet silence, what little of it Diggory saw. Wearied with journeying, and wandering, and heartache, he could not watch it through, as he'd planned, and await the return of Maut; he fell asleep.

It was Maut, though, that woke him, pounding on his door; he opened it to find her standing there, the sun still tangled in her hair, and a wildness about her, but Maut still. 'Diggory!' said she, beaming, and a squirrel ran down her skirt and shot through the half-open door. He heard its claws skittering over the wood-grown floor behind him. 'Here you are, sound asleep at home, like a sensible man; I ought to have known.'

This cut too close for his liking, bringing all the fears of yester eve back to his mind. His smile was small. Still, Maut was here: Mother had been right. 'What brings you back, Maut? Or is it Mauvian?'

She blinked at him. 'Where else should I be, pray, but here? I'm going home. I've a mind to rest a bit myself, for there's to be carousing this night, and I'll need my strength. Here.' She showed him a delicate thing of spider-lace, or some such stuff: silver-limned, an inscription glimmered there. 'The Moon-Queen and her brother!' said Maut, laughing and shaking her head. 'Or, as we know him, *Gower Bordekin,* all with his finery on. They're to celebrate tonight, with a grand feast. Such splendour. Not perfectly to my taste, Diggory, nor yours either, I'll be bound, but since I'm famished enough to eat half the forest my own self, I'm minded to go. Besides, all the folk will be there.'

'The folk?' said Diggory, dazed, taking the scraplet of cobweb-silk and blinking at it. 'Which folk?'

'The folk of the Tree,' said Maut, with a touch of impatience, and pushed her way past him into the round bole of his house. 'Brackenberry's to go, of course — nothing could keep *him* away. Mudling's promised, and Willow-Wild, and Gower of course. Mother Merigot, and the Tree, and you, and me.'

'Me?' echoed Diggory. 'What, am I to go to a royal feast?'

Maut, noticing at last the odd way about him, folded her arms, and stared. 'What, has the dust got into your brains, Diggory? What can you mean? Of course you're to go.'

'I haven't had one of these.' He waved the silvery thing, a mulish expression hiding the sinking of his heart.

'*That* is for you. I've another. Here.' She pulled a second, matching summons from a fold in her tunic, and brandished it at him. '*That* one you're holding, you'd have found it yourself if you'd got up sooner. 'Twas wafting about outside your door. The Tree kept an eye on it, I'll be bound, or it would have blown away long since.'

'Oh.'

'Take good care of it, too, for I've a fancy the lady put some labour into it.' She winked, and turned to go. 'You've a better suit to wear than that old jerkin, I trust?'

'No.' Diggory knew a moment's doubt, but this soon cleared away. 'I'll go as I am. If I'm not welcome like this, I shan't be the more so for a velvet doublet.'

'That's good sense.' Maut smiled at him. 'As ever.

We flighty folk have need of a Diggory Stokey, don't we? What a mess we'd get ourselves into, without.'

'Seems to me that's just what happened,' said Diggory, a smile tugging at the corners of his mouth. 'Mayhap I'd better stay a while. Just to keep an eye on things, you know.'

Maut, surprisingly, crossed the floor again, and planted a sound kiss on his face. The changes in her were not only physical: it was as though the sun had gone out of her, long ago, and now it was back again. She glowed. 'Sleep, for me,' she said. 'I'll see you at moon's rise. Bring your dancing feet, Diggory.' She went out again in a whirl of sunlight, and the squirrels pelted after her.

Diggory, smiling, went back to bed. If the lady's wisp of thistle-silk went under his pillow, I'm sure there's none to blame him.

Picture, then, the days that followed! And the nights, too, for there it began: in the velvet moss of the lady's bower, moonlight lighting the faces and bared arms of her Court. She, resplendent upon her throne (for a little while), her brother, proud and tall, beside her. Imagine the music: a feast for the ears, that, a medley of silver pipes and drums; of dulcet harps strung with rainwater, melodies rippling like the river; of stamping feet and voices raised in songs, the like of which had not been heard under those dreaming eaves for a hundred years.

There were almond-tarts for her Majesty, and sweet marchpane, and apple-wine. There were rosewater dainties, leaf-wrapped loaves stuffed with wild herbs gathered from the riverbank. There were pitchers of clear water, drawn from still, forest lakes under the noon sun. Every delicacy the Court of

Summertide could wish for lay spread over silken cloths under the moon; and by the dawn, little remained.

The folk of the Tree slipped seamlessly into this thicket of fey; even Diggory Stokey, for after a goblet or two of apple-wine (and the soft touch of the Moon-Queen's lips upon his cheek, a profound magic to Diggory's mind), he forgot that there had ever been troubles fancied, in his own mind, or others'. He was as fey as the rest of them, that night, full of roses and wine, and almond-tarts; he danced and sang with as much abandon as Brackenberry, or Willow-Wild, and never again would he call himself a stranger in the forest.

Gowerlon Summer-King had arrived on the back of Nynlath the dragon; this irascible soul spent the feast with his long body wrapped around the trunk of the Kottow-Tree. He was fed with marchpane from Quince's own, fair hands; plied with lake-water and wine; and welcomed the dawn with a mist all his own, a goldish smoke that poured from his flared nostrils, and hung heavy upon the air, lighting the queen's bower with a burnished glow as the sun rose.

And when, shortly before dawn, a latecomer appeared, they were, all of them, too merry to mind; nobody was going to fear the Winter, now.

'I've brought wine,' said Berengaria, appearing under the verdant eaves with nothing of fanfare about her. And though she *did* have a crown nestled in the coils of her hair, a cold-glittering thing with the look of ice about it, she wore besides the same linen gown she'd been wont to wear in Kottow. 'I am sorry, it's a little cold — I cannot seem to help that, now.'

The cold came in with her, this was true, but only

a slow chill, low to the ground; no bitter blast of killing Winter to trouble the feast-goers, and nobody minded it at all.

MORE STORIES BY CHARLOTTE E. ENGLISH:

THE WONDER TALES:

Faerie Fruit
Gloaming
Sands and Starlight
Summertide

THE TALES OF AYLFENHAME:

Miss Landon and Aubranael
Miss Ellerby and the Ferryman
Bessie Bell and the Goblin King
Mr. Drake and My Lady Silver

www.charlotteenglish.com

Made in United States
North Haven, CT
05 July 2022

20973623R00136